SHOW BUSINESS

SHOW BUSINESS
A MYSTERY NOVEL

BRYANT FORD

COACHWHIP PUBLICATIONS
Greenville, Ohio

The characters and incidents in this book are strictly
fictitious. If any characters resemble real people it
is not the author's fault.

Show Business, by Bryant Ford (pseud.)
© 2017 Coachwhip Publications

Title published 1939
Michael Blankfort (1907-1982)
No claims made on public domain material.

Front cover: Pattern © Ifh85

CoachwhipBooks.com

ISBN 1-61646-400-3
ISBN-13 978-1-61646-400-4

ABOUT THE AUTHOR

Bryant Ford was a pseudonym for novelist, playwright, and screenwriter Michael Blankfort (1907-1982). Though a prolific writer, *Show Business* (1939) was the only time he used this pen name. Under his own name he wrote such thrillers as *The Widow-Makers*, *The Juggler*, and *I Met a Man*. In Hollywood, his numerous film credits included *The Plainsman*, *The Juggler*, *The Caine Mutiny*, and *Tribute to a Bad Man*.

    Show Business was published by Dodd, Mead as a Red Badge Detective novel.

SHOW BUSINESS

TO JERRY AND LARRY
WHO NEVER MURDERED
A MAN OR PRODUCED A PLAY—
AND, I HOPE, NEVER WILL

CHAPTER I
"I HAVE SO FEW FRIENDS"

The leaves were turning brown in Westchester County, but actors were getting jobs in New York. People were shaking camphor flakes off the shoulders of their topcoats, the football heroes ran superlative touchdowns in Friday's sport columns, and Broadway's show business was awakening from its summer torpor with all the subtle excitement of an extinct lizard breathing again after a thousand years' sleep. This was fall. This was new shows, new jobs, new billboards, new crowds . . . new money.

From the Empire Theater on 40th Street to the Theatre Guild on 52nd Street, Broadway twisted in the grip of its perennial resurgence. From the corniest honky-tonks and flea circuses on 42nd Street to the latest redrafting of Shakespeare by the Mercury Theater, the thousand craftsmen of the sad and comic muses looked out from the kennels of their summer sleep, took a sniff at the cool, charged air, and began drawing up budgets, buying options, hiring actors, renting theaters, slap-happying drama editors, ferreting out angels, rehearsing, wheedling, and cursing their compatriots with the venom which only blood brothers can pour out on each other.

Broadway has a chambermaid's ear and a spinster's tongue. It's as crude as a Mack truck and as sensitive as *Suite for Flutes and Orchestra* by Bach. It's got sin and sacrifice, greed, generosity and genius. In short, it's pretty much like everything else.

Billy Rose is only a magnified small-town county fair impresario, and Walter Winchell is no more nor less than the society

columnist on the West Stayon *Clarion* who records how the Miss-
es Whitcomb threw a fudge-making party last Wednesday after a
church social.

Bill Benedict glanced from a 24 sheet billboard tastefully announc-
ing the new Leo Murray production of *Hour's End* to a Western
Union clock in a ticket broker's window. It was ten o'clock. He
checked his own old-fashioned Ingersoll which he had been carrying
ever since he graduated from De Witt Clinton High School over in
Hell's Kitchen.

He sniffed the fall air and started his daily walk to Leo Murray's office.

Bill, whose thin, well-dressed form, dark, curly hair and long
nose were as much a Broadway landmark as Grover Whalen's
gardenia, didn't really have to look at a clock to know the time.
Broadway inhabitants were like farmers in this respect. They
could tell time just by looking at the people on the street. Before
noon, there were mostly workers or unemployed musicians—or
kid actors who had not yet learned that the best time to see
a producer was between five and six in the evening. On matinee
days, they knew it was two o'clock by the determined crowds of
women who pushed their way around Leblang's like ants fighting over a dead fly. At two-thirty, the same women rushed north-
ward along the street dodging traffic and knocking down idlers
in a nervous effort to beat curtain time. There was a different
crowd between three and five; different in pocketbook and dress.
The Paramount or Roxy or Radio City crowds. Late afternoon,
the matinee molls would be skeltering toward the south; and, at
six, the office workers avalanched down on the pavements and
squirmed along for the subways.

Bill knew all these signs like an Indian. Unlike an Indian, he
enjoyed the knowledge. It made him feel good and wise.

Bill got in the elevator of the Regent Theater Building on 48th
Street between Broadway and Eighth Avenue. Angus, the Negro
elevator man, greeted him with an amiable grin.

"Hya, Mr. Benedict."

"Hya, Angus."

"Wanta make a little jack, Mr. Benedict?"

"How come?"

"Mr. Murray's openin' his eleventh show tonight, ain't he?"

"Yeah."

"Every single one of 'em was a smasheroo, waren't it?"

"If it's a Leo Murray production, it's a hit. You know that, Angus."

Angus smiled happily. "I sure do. That's why I'm gonna make some dough on this one."

"Leo let you buy in?"

"No such luck."

"Then where are you going to make your jack?"

"Playin' number 11 in today's policy. It's gotta hit. I'll get 600–1 if I get a cent. I know it like I know today's Tuesday."

"Watch out the District Attorney don't get you."

"No, suh!"

The fourth floor had been reached long before this. Angus opened the door.

"Put a buck on it for me," said Bill.

There was nice discreet lettering on the office door.

Mr. Leo Murray
Leo Murray Productions

Francis Xavier Boley,
Mr. Murray's General Manager

William Benedict,
Mr. Murray's Press Representative

Bill pushed his way inside. The office was filled with actors looking for work. Ruth, Leo's sister, was at the reception desk reading a script. She wore a tailor-made suit but had a gentle, sensitive way of handling herself. She was the most popular turner-awayer on Broadway and had a nose for good plays. Leo counted a good deal on her judgment. But he never admitted it.

"Any calls, Ruthie?" asked Bill.

"Herbert Bayard Swope's secretary called for press tickets."

"Send 'em out. He's always good for a note in Winchell."

"The D.A.'s office called for two."

"Okay."

"Valenti'll have the pictures up here at noon. Zolotow of the *Times* called to know whether there's been a broker's buy. . . ."

"The hell with that."

"Sue Huxley of the *Examiner* wants you to call her."

"Now, for Chrissake, Ruthie. That's the important call!"

Ruth smiled. "Why don't you marry her, and get her off the phone?"

"I got to have something to fill my day with. Will you get her for me, Ruthie?"

"Little cupid, Ruthie." She plugged the board and dialed the *Examiner* number. "I ought to go around with a bunch of arrows."

"It wouldn't hurt you if you got one stuck in yourself. Somebody's got to carry the Murray dynasty along."

Ruth pulled the plug out abruptly. "Line's busy, Bill." She didn't look at him.

"No feelings hurt?"

"Go to hell," Ruth said softly. She turned to where some W.P.A. actors were sitting in wait for Leo Murray. "Listen, kids. For the tenth time I tell you, no one can see Mr. Murray today. Now, beat it, please. If you leave your names and addresses we'll call you when we cast again."

Bill walked down the dark corridor toward his office. The place was built like a railroad flat with a dust-infested hall linking Ruth's outer office with the untouchable precincts of Leo Murray's. And jutting out from the hall like square knobs were Bill's office and Boley's with a toilet between the two.

"Hya, Frank." Bill had to pass Boley's office to get to his own. He stuck his head inside to greet him.

Boley nodded. He was smoking and his hands were busy. In his right, he held a bottle of Haig and Haig, and in his other was a Lily cup. Boley, for the last twenty-five years, had lived, it seemed, solely on the calories and vitamins found in good Scotch and twenty-five cent cigars. He looked like a prosperous Tammany ward-heeler.

Bill went into his own office, closed the door, lit a cigarette and pulled out a copy of Hemingway he had hidden behind a pile of *Varietys*. Hemingway could write a good book on show business if he ever got around to it.

The phone rang. It was Ruthie.

"*Daily Worker's* calling," she said.

"What do they want?"

"Press tickets for tonight."

"Who the hell they think they are? Got a circulation of a couple thousand Communists and they want press tickets to a Leo Murray opening. Tell 'em no."

"Don't forget the second act, Bill."

"What about it?"

Ruth sounded a warning. "It's got social significance."

Bill sighed.

"If the carriage trade gets sore we'll have to pull for the straphangers, The New School, Carnegie Hall, and the Union Square crowd." She paused. "It might be *only* an artistic success."

"Send them second night tickets. . . . And, Ruthie, keep trying the *Examiner*." He hung up.

Boley's phone rang. Boley said:

"Thanks, Ruth." He threw his whisky-wet Lily cups in the wastepaper basket and hid the bottle of Scotch in his desk.

Then Bill's phone rang.

"Leo's come in," Ruth said.

Bill started to make sounds on his typewriter.

Leo walked softly for a man. There was a short silence, then:

"Good morning, Leo," Boley said expansively.

"Did they hang the new floodlight last night?"

There was a pause. "Yes," Boley said.

Leo came up to Bill's door. "I want to see you in a couple of minutes."

Bill nodded. When Leo went into his own office, slamming the door behind him, Bill pulled the sheet of paper out of his typewriter and crumpled it in a sudden angry gesture. "He makes you feel like a piece of disposable tissue," he muttered.

He waited five minutes and went into Leo's office. He stood at the door. Leo was reading the morning paper.

"What do you want, Leo?"

Leo turned over a page and made some markings with a pencil. His small dark sardonic head was bowed over the sheet.

"You said for me to come in."

"Don't stand up there like the Statue of Liberty."

Leo hated anybody taller than he was. Bill grinned and remained standing.

The telephone rang. Leo picked up the receiver and listened. Then: "Tell him I don't want his lousy play. . . . I don't care what I promised. He says he counted on me? Tell him next time to count on the weather." He hung up and went back to his paper.

"I got work to do, Leo."

The producer stared at him with nervous dark eyes. "Sit down."

Bill shrugged and pulled over a hard chair. He sat on it.

Leo stood up and walked over to Bill. He looked down at him. "Heard what Finley's saying?"

"No."

"He says I robbed him of *Hour's End*."

"Nick's always griping."

Leo suddenly became compassionate: "His envy'll kill him."

"He's a joker, Leo. He accused Max Reinhardt of stealing *The Miracle* right out of his pants pocket."

"I want it stopped."

"Why don't you see a good lawyer?"

Leo paced up and down in front of Bill.

"Try buying him off," Bill said.

"Not a cent. Not if I knew I was going to make a million."

"What do you want me to do?" Bill asked. "And keep it clean."

Leo brushed some dust off the arm of his blue suit. It was his favorite. It had up and down stripes to help his height.

"Get the columnists to run some stories that Nick won't like. How he stole my first angel from me."

"The boys don't like libel."

Leo reddened. "I'll go to court and swear it's true."

Bill laughed aloud. "*You'll* go to court? What do you think I am, a harp from the Ould Sod? Maybe you've forgotten that you lost my private detective license for me because you wouldn't go near a court. 'Below your dignity,' you said."

"Now . . . Bill . . ." Leo made a conciliatory movement of his slender fingers.

"Hell! If you'd've testified that I had broken into Graham's apartment only to get your letters back, I'd still be earning an honest living instead of pandering paragraphs about Leo Murray's genius."

Leo smiled. He felt flattered. Then his sardonic lips tightened. "You hate me, don't you, Bill?"

"Yes."

"But you respect me."

"Yes."

"That's all I want. The minute you don't respect me, I'll know. Then I fire you."

"Why confess?"

The phone rang. "Leo Murray talking. . . . I'm not interested in farces. I don't care if it's the best thing you have to offer. . . . All right, send it over to the Theatre Guild. Maybe they'll get O'Neill to rewrite." He hung the receiver back in place and stared moodily at a picture on the wall of a scene from his Pulitzer Prize play. He walked over to Bill. "There I go, insulting another agent."

"Why?"

"Because I tell the truth about the way I feel, and you got to salve people."

"I mean why confess to me?"

"Because everybody's ganging up on me. Nick and Charlie Beach and the agents. Broadway all rolled up in a package. My taste, they hate. My success, they call luck. They can't stand something well done in the theater."

"They do pretty well by themselves."

"I give Broadway its best shows. Real stuff. No can-can. No lousy movie farces. I work with the writers. I make something out of the lousy scripts they bring in. Actresses. They don't know how to walk. They don't know what to do with their hands. I teach them. Directors. I let them watch me and learn. Every one of them hates me."

"Where do I come in?"

"Do a job with the papers."

"You get your name in," Bill said.

"Don't make it sound cheap. I want credit only for my own work." Leo strode across the room angrily. "I want it understood by everybody that a Leo Murray production means everything Leo Murray from script to lighting to acting. I want them to be proud to have me rewrite their plays for them."

Bill looked at Leo and narrowed his eyes. He got up slowly and walked to the door. "What you need is Ivy Lee," he said.

Leo opened a letter wearily. "I have so few friends. A man goes under unless he fights for himself." He shook his head.

Bill closed the door with a sharp click.

Ruth was trying to persuade the jobless actors that Leo wouldn't see them. "Not if you were Maurice Evans' father or Katherine Cornell in mufti," she said. The door leading from the elevator opened. It was Charlie Beach.

Charlie was as slim as a Ry-Krisp ad. A nervous and maladjusted thyroid bulged his eyes out like a couple of loose black buttons.

"I want to see Leo."

"He's not in." Ruth said.

"I want to see Leo," he repeated coldly, keeping his eyes on the back of her neck.

"I'm sorry, Charlie."

"Tie it up and throw it away!"

"He'll be back at five."

"I'll wait for him in his office." Charlie swung open the gate leading into the hall.

Ruth made no move to stop him. She called Leo on the inter-office phone. "Charlie Beach is coming in." She was apologetic.

Leo scowled, poured some water out of a silver pitcher, sipped it and waited.

Charlie entered the office and closed the door carefully. Leo arose from his chair.

"You can sit down again, Leo. I know what you look like standing."

The producer hesitated; then sat on the corner of his desk. He cleared his throat. He smiled amicably. "What's clouding up your day, Charlie?"

Beach pressed his lips together, annoyed. "Why did you take my name off the house boards and programs?"

Leo relaxed. "Read any good new plays recently?" he asked.

"Why did you take my name off?"

Leo shrugged hopelessly and walked toward the window. "If you think it'll do you any good to have it on—"

"I deserve it."

"That's open to interpretation."

"I worked on the show for two and a half weeks. I thought up the second-act curtain. I fixed it so the exits in the first were clear. I deserve it." Charlie's eyes were watering in anger.

Leo fiddled with the telephone. Then he smiled with a martyr's irony. "Broadway knows that no one contributes to any show I produce but me. They'll praise me and laugh at you." He took a step forward. "You damn fool! I took your name off as a favor to you!"

Beach smiled in a mirthless way. His doughy face stretched grimly. "It's an old trick of yours, Leo, putting people on the defensive." He chuckled. "Makes me feel I owe you something."

Leo tapped on his desk impatiently. "I know more about these things than you do, Charlie."

"If my name isn't on the house boards and programs tonight," Charlie said evenly, "you'll have a premiere you won't forget."

Leo smiled sadly. "Need any dough, Charlie?"

Charlie kept his eyes on Leo.

"Eddie Mannix of M.G.M. is coming to town tomorrow," Leo continued. "Maybe there's a job for you. Dialogue director." He took some bills out of his pocket and put them on the corner of the desk near Charlie. "Take it, kid. And forget about paying it back."

The bulging eyes dropped to the money, then were raised back to Leo's swarthy face. Charlie took a step toward the producer. He picked up the money. He tore the bills in two and threw them in Leo's face. "You'll have a premiere you won't forget, Leo." He walked out.

Murray wiped his face slowly as if the money had been wet. He wasn't angry; he felt elated. He stood in the slab of sunlight that jutted from the window and breathed deeply once or twice. Then he dialed Ruth. "Send Benedict in."

Bill came in. Leo pointed to the torn money on the floor. "Take those bills over to the bank. Get them exchanged for good ones." Bill hesitated a moment. But he bent down and gathered up the pieces of paper.

"Charlie Beach was in to see me," Leo said in a pained voice. "He's a maniac, that man. Delusions of grandeur. A homicidal paranoiac. I feel sorry for him. Don't you?" Bill nodded. "Failure to some men is like poison. He has big ideas, no guts." Murray rubbed his hands against each other thoughtfully. "A Hollywood job will keep him off my neck."

"Hollywood gets rid of a lot of good people," Bill said.

"People are inverted. Help them; they hate you. Despise them and they respect you." He paused. "Someone ought to write a book about the physiology of social relations."

"Bring the bills back here?" Bill asked.

"In every group of men, one is the energizing heart. He sends out the good, fresh, aerated red blood. Do you know your physiology, Bill?"

"Charlie deserves a break."

"You know what the heart gets back? The diseased and used-up blood, the tired, painful dark fluid." He ran a hand wearily over his eyes. "Go to the bank, Bill," he sighed. "I feel like being alone."

"You got a lot of ionized gall, Leo," Bill said and walked out.

Ruth finally was able to get a connection at the *Examiner* and told Bill that Sue Huxley was on the wire.

"Hell, Huxley," Bill shouted sweetly into the phone. "You're harder to get than four stars from Burns Mantle. Will you be in your office in an hour or will I have to swear out a warrant to see you?"

"After all, the *Examiner* pays me to see press agents," Sue replied.

"Okay, sweetheart. I love you."

"Very well, Mr. Benedict." Sue became distant. "Someone from the *Examiner* will undoubtedly cover Mr. Murray's opening." She hung up.

Bill decided that if *Hour's End* was a smash (which he suspected it wouldn't be) he would ask Leo for a raise and marry the girl.

At ten minutes to eleven, Ruth left her desk and entered Leo Murray's office.

"What do you want? I didn't ring for you," he said harshly.

Ruth sighed unhappily. "God, Leo, I never quite get used to your crudeness. Sometimes, I pity you."

Leo laughed.

"It's time for your rehearsal."

"I know it's time." He stepped toward her and looked at her appraisingly. "Why don't you take care of yourself, Ruth? I give you enough money to dress better. Why don't you get your hair washed and set once in a while?"

Ruth flushed and ran her hand across her hair. "It's not true. You're lying. You don't give me enough money. You're just talking because you have to find some excuse to justify yourself."

"People'll say I don't support my sister," he continued ironically. His slender fingers moved constantly when he was upset. Ruth concentrated on them. "And never let Charlie Beach in to see me again."

"I couldn't help it."

"Call a cop next time. The man threatened to kill me."

"I'll tell Angus not to take him up on the elevator."

"What if he walks up, you damned fool!"

"All right, Leo. I'll take care of it. Now go to your rehearsal."

He walked over to her. "You're a sweet one, Ruth," he said without irony. He patted her cheek. He took his hat and walked out. A look of deep gratification covered Ruth's face.

CHAPTER 11
THE LADY WHO PLAYED A LOUSE

Leo and Bill walked along Broadway toward 45th Street. They were heading for the Arcadia Theater. At a Nedick's stand Leo stopped for an orange drink.

"Doctor says I got to get more vitamins."

They crossed Shubert alley.

Lee Shubert, brown as earth, was just getting out of his Rolls Royce as they passed.

"Good luck, Leo," Lee said in his whispering voice.

"Thanks, Lee."

"But you'd've done better, Leo, if you'd have come into one of my theaters."

"Next time. Maybe."

The Arcadia Theater was one of the oldest houses on Broadway. The hundreds of plays which mellowed its stage had given it a Stradivarius uniqueness. The audiences who came to the Arcadia expected a dignified drama. No one would think of putting on a farce at the Arcadia. It just didn't fit. The dusty draperies, the gilt-painted boxes and balcony demanded artistic respectability from the stage. Rehearsals, however, made it look like a frowsy Louis Quatorze countess after a hard night of debauch. The glaring, unshaded stage light threw uncomfortable shadows back into the auditorium, turning the gilt crapulous and the thin plush of the chairs bumpy.

Leo and Bill entered the theater and were effusively greeted by Sentineal, the Negro doorman. They saw before them on the stage Ricky Linton, the stage manager, sprawled out on a property couch reading a copy of *Spur*. Standing near him was Sir Basil Gilbert, a C. Aubrey Smith-looking British actor especially imported for *Hour's End*, reading his lines quietly to himself. Center stage Steve Levy, Ricky's assistant, yelled orders to the stage electrician.

"Come down a point on that No. 2 bastard amber," Steve was saying.

"Hey, Steve!" Leo yelled.

Steve turned and shielded his eyes against the stage light glare.

"Good morning, Mr. Murray."

"What are you doing with that bastard amber?"

"Bringing it down a bit."

"What for?"

Steve took off his glasses and polished them for a moment in silence.

"You heard me, Steve. What for?" Leo repeated quietly.

"Because that's what you ordered."

Leo's face paled a little.

"Excuses! Now change it back to where it was." Steve put on his glasses and called up to the

electrician. "Okay, Andy, leave that No. 2 alone." Leo walked on stage and nodded to Sir Basil who was obviously annoyed by Leo's manner.

"Linton!" Leo snapped out the name.

Ricky Linton rose from the couch, slammed the magazine down on the floor, stared disinterestedly at Leo and went off stage right.

"I'd like to squash that son-of-a-bitch," he murmured as he passed Andy at the switchboard.

"You ain't the only one, son," Andy replied.

"Everybody on stage, Steve," Leo ordered.

"Miss Lawrence hasn't come in yet."

"So. . . . Miss Lawrence doesn't take my rehearsals seriously. Go out and call her hotel. Tell her if she's not here in ten minutes . . ."

"Good morning, Mr. Murray."

Leo turned to face Alice Lawrence.

"You're late," he said.

"My fault, Murray," said MacMonnies, who had entered with the actress. He was a tall, slim, blond man with a face that matched the white linen handkerchief in his breast-pocket.

"Naturally," said Leo. "But unfortunately, we need Miss Lawrence. It's she who has to appear tonight, not you. A playwright has no business disrupting rehearsals."

"Sorry," said MacMonnies coldly. "It's my business as much as yours."

"Everybody on stage," Leo yelled.

The cast lined up.

"Places for Act Three, Scene Three," Leo said curtly.

"Act Three, Scene Three please," Steve repeated. Ricky Linton was nowhere around.

Alice Lawrence took her place upstage in the country home set. Downstage right of her stood Nina Gale, a dark, beautiful girl who played Alice's younger sister. Making the third point to the triangle was Sir Basil Gilbert.

"Ready?"

The actors nodded.

"Curtain."

The large, dark red curtain fell slowly.

"House lights out," yelled Leo.

The house became dark. A signal buzzed and the curtain rose. Alice Lawrence started the scene.

> ALICE:
> *I know the truth. (She crosses to Sir Basil) The truth
> is you love my sister.*
> SIR BASIL:
> *(Clasping his hands behind him) It's the truth as you
> see it, my dear.*
> NINA:
> *(To Alice) Darling, you mustn't be outspoken. After
> all, if your lover finds me attractive—*
> ALICE:
> *Stop it.*

NINA:

I'm young.

SIR BASIL:

If you don't mind, I'll leave you two alone.

ALICE:

Cowardice and infidelity make cozy bed partners.

SIR BASIL:

That's unfair.

NINA:

(Singing) Everything in love and war. . . .

ALICE:

(After a moment's reflection) Yes. You're right, my dear sister, you are right. I am the vanquished and you are the victor. (Very sympathetically) Why shouldn't you take my lover from me? Let him teach you the pain of beauty, and the beauty of pain.

"Wait a minute, wait a minute!" Leo cried. He strode down the aisle. "Who changed those lines?"

No one spoke.

"I said who changed those lines?"

"I did," MacMonnies said.

"What for?"

"Because I think it strengthens the scene."

"Don't you mean you think it makes Miss Lawrence more sympathetic?"

"Maybe it does."

"That's the way it should be," Alice added.

"I say no! It's not the way it's going to be in my production."

Alice leaned over the footlights. "Why don't you want me to be sympathetic? The part can stand it."

"What are the original lines, Steve?" Leo asked.

Steve looked into his prompt book. "After Julie says, 'Everything in love and war' Miss Lawrence's speech is: 'You're right. My dear sister, you're right. I am the vanquished and you are the victor. But my lover will sell you as cheaply as he has sold me.'"

"That's the way it's going to be," said Leo.

"Why do you want to make me a louse?" Alice asked bitterly.

"Because you play one so well."

No one saw Ricky come on stage and jump from the apron to the floor. He leaned down and slammed a fist into Leo's face. Leo cried out and fell. Steve and Bill Benedict pulled Ricky away.

Leo got up slowly. His face was white.

"Steve." His voice trembled slightly. "If those lines are not the way I want them tonight, bring down the curtain. Those are my orders." Then he turned to Alice Lawrence and bowed imperceptibly. "I apologize." He sounded very humble. "I apologize to the rest of you," he continued. "The important thing now is that we all work together to put this play across the best way we know how." He sighed. "Now, let's start all over again. Places for Act Three, Scene Three."

"Act Three, Scene Three," Steve reiterated in a mumble. "Curtain."

The curtain fell cumbrously and the house lights darkened. Backstage, behind the shell of the set-flats, a quiet little poker game had been organized by Andy, the chief electrician. Undisturbed by the sound of the actors' voices, and watching Andy as he dealt the first round, were two prop men, Abe Feldman and Danny Hara, and a grip, "Dutch" Schultz, a meek little Yankee whose real name was Obadiah Prescott, and a fifth man who was a stranger to the others. He had been sent there by Local 22 as a grip. The name his union card carried was Phil Dillon. He was stocky, blue-eyed, unsmiling, and didn't know a stage-brace from a pair of suspenders. No one liked him.

The first four hands passed off without undue excitement. "Dutch" Schultz, who kept protesting that he couldn't play poker, won six dollars the first deal by bluffing with a pair of openers. The second deal went to Danny Hara, who drew to a full house. The third and fourth deals piled the chips up in front of "Dutch."

"I don't understand it, boys," he said apologetically.

"The luck of the innocent," Hara commented sourly.

Phil Dillon began dealing the fifth round.

Andy lit a cigar. "This cookie, Murray," he said to no one in particular, "is a pain."

"With deuces wild," Abe Feldman added.

Danny Hara started to say something and stopped. He shifted on his seat imperceptibly so he could get a closer look at Dillon.

Andy picked up his second card; they were playing five card stud. "I heard him tell Steve to dim down on that Number 2 bastard amber, and here he comes in, changes his mind, and bawls the pants off the kid. A stinker, that's what he is."

Dillon's eyes fluttered as if something had flown in them. Quickly, he wiped his sleeve across his face. Hara bit his lips and moved his chair closer to Dillon. He suddenly felt a pressure on his leg under the table. He looked around. "Dutch" was winking at him.

Abe Feldman fiddled with his cards. "I bet Murray," he whispered hoarsely to Andy, "wakes up in the morning and finds his hands around his own throat. You know—he takes a cop with him when he goes to the bank. He don't trust himself."

The others laughed.

"Not so loud," Andy warned.

The deal was over. Everybody looked at his cards. Hara suddenly threw his in the middle of the table, reached over and pulled Dillon's cards out of his hand.

Dillon shot up from the table. He had a gun in his hand. The smile on his face wasn't pretty. "What'samatter, Mister?" he said to Hara evenly. "Don't ya like it here?"

"You dealt from the bottom of the deck," Hara said.

Dillon's eyes shifted slowly around the table from face to face. "Anybody else see me?"

No one spoke. Andy tongued his cigar and put it down distastefully.

Dillon chuckled. "That's funny. No one else saw me."

Hara began to sweat. Then "Dutch" said in a frightened twang, "Me. I saw you cheat."

"Okay. That's makes two. Now, what're ya gonna do about it?"

There was a split-second pause. Hara moved quickly and slapped Dillon's hand. The gun fell to the floor. Hara and Feldman jumped for it. Dillon smashed a fist into Hara's face and kicked Feldman in the back. Andy picked up a chair.

"Put it down," said Dillon. The gun was back in his hand. His blue eyes were darkened for an instant and what might have passed for a smile in another man flickered on his lips. Then they opened narrowly. "You dumb bastards." He backed slowly toward the fire door. "Which one of you guys socked the rod outta my hands?" He looked coldly from one to the other; his eyes finally rested on Hara. He lifted the gun.

"Laney!"

Dillon's hand wavered. Bill had come in.

"For Chrissake, Laney!" Bill walked over to Dillon. "I thought you were dead."

Dillon didn't smile. He shifted the gun from Hara to Bill. Bill side-stepped quickly as he shoved his foot in Dillon's abdomen. The gun went off. Bill knifed the back of his hand into Dillon's neck. The gun dropped to the floor.

"Let's quit, Laney," Bill said. He walked over to Dillon and put his arm in his. "I thought you were dead. Where were you St. Valentine's day in Chicago? I could've sworn the boys had taken you over for good."

Dillon said nothing. He wiped his lips mechanically and stared oddly at Bill.

Bill turned to Andy. "What the hell's the idea of palling up with a rat like Laney?"

"He ain't no pal," Andy protested. "Local 22 sent him over as a grip."

"Let's see your union card," Bill said. Laney gave it to him. Bill laughed, "Dillon, eh? No more Dillon than I am." He turned to Andy. "He put something over on you, boys."

Andy patted Feldman. "Call up 22 and find out what's the idea of sending gorillas out with a card."

Leo Murray swaggered across the stage. "What's giving out here? Can't a man have a quiet rehearsal?"

Andy explained.

"Who said you could play cards on my time?" Leo demanded. "If you were gypped, it serves you right." He turned to Bill. "Make a note. I'm taking this up with the union."

"Keep your tie in, Leo," Bill said. "There's nothing in the union agreement that says the boys can't play cards if they have nothing to do. Besides, this Laney doll didn't come here to collect some small change." Bill walked close to Laney. "Unless he's reformed." Laney flickered a smile. "Nope," Bill continued. "You didn't reform, Laney. There isn't a prison system in the world that could do anything to you except put calluses on your behind." The smile left Laney's lips.

"What's he here for then?" Leo asked.

"Answer him, Laney," Bill said.

Laney thought a minute. "I t'ought you was a big-shot copper by now, Benny."

"We're not talking about me," Bill said. "But if it'll help, I'll tell you. I'm a press agent now. I'm earning an honest living."

The gangster grinned. "Me too."

"That ain't funny."

Steve Levy pushed his way through the group. "Shall I call the cops, Bill?" he asked.

Bill looked Laney up and down. He noticed that the man was wearing new clothes. He smiled thoughtfully. "Who's keeping you, Laney?" The man didn't answer. "I got a soft spot in my head for you, guy. I'm not going to let 'em call the cops this time."

"Are you crazy?" Leo yelled.

Bill ignored him and continued, "But if I see you around here again, I'm going to do more than turn you over to the cops. I'm going to deliver you—on a morgue table. Beat it!"

Laney picked up his gun.

"By the way, Laney," Bill said pleasantly, "we're going to have a lot of cops here opening night. If you like cops, come around."

Laney left without answering.

Bill walked over to Leo and put his arm in his. "No, I'm not crazy, friend. I'm just all-wise. Come into a dressing room. I want to talk to you."

CHAPTER III
"EVERY MAN HATES HIS MASTER"

Bill Benedict left Leo at the rehearsal and snagged a Seventh Avenue subway to the *Examiner's* offices. Office boys fell before him like weeds under a tractor. He entered Susan Huxley's drama-editor cubby with a whistle on his lips.

"Huxley!"

"Nice going, Benedict." She looked up. "The boss'll knock me over like a ten-pin if you come in sounding off like that. Why don't you get yourself a nice quiet calliope instead?"

"Huxley, I love you."

"Excuse me, Mr. B," said Sue. "I'm not buying any." She ignored his lips briefly by tapping her own against his cheek and went on opening a package which lay on her desk.

"It's a bomb. I sent it to you," said Bill.

Sue tore the last tissue piece off the package. "It's perfume."

Bill scratched his nose. "I didn't send it."

"I know," Sue sighed. "The only presents I ever get from you are press releases on Leo Murray shows."

"Save 'em, Huxley. I autograph for a consideration."

"My God!" Sue exclaimed.

"What's the matter? A blackhand note?"

Sue's eyes were angry. She showed him a card tied on the bottle. "Don't say it."

"It's from Don Lankershim. He writes as follows, the lug. 'Dear, dear Sue. Use this perfume but don't forget to use a double spread picture of Cutie Cunard, my latest client. Many thanks. Don Lankershim.'"

"Stout fella."

"And I've always wanted this kind of perfume," Sue said ruefully.

"Why not use it?"

"Me take graft?"

"No." He picked up the bottle and sniffed at it. "Just use it and don't give him the spread. That's not graft; that's gravy. Just a present from an admirer."

"You got something there, Bill." Sue dialed the composing room. "Hey, Fred. Yank that double column photo of Cutie Cunard. Yes. . . . I'll send something else down right away." She hung up and smiled at Bill.

"You had it in already?"

She nodded.

"But it wouldn't have been graft. You got the perfume *after* you decided to use his picture."

"It's the principle. A lady's got to keep her virtue. Before or after. Which reminds me, Charlie Beach called up to announce that he's going to appear at the opening of *Hour's End* tonight and raise a stink. Why don't you work for a decent boss?"

"Leo was born with a silver knife in his back. How about dinner tonight?" Bill straightened his tie.

"You're a coward. If you don't like someone why work for him?"

"If you like someone, why not marry him?"

She waved him away. "I'm busy. Besides, you're a parasite of the people, a lackey of the kept press, a molehill on the buttocks of Time."

"What the hell you talking about?" he demanded.

"Oh . . ." She flicked ashes off a cigarette airily. "I'm getting all worked up for the proletarian drama I'm going to cover tonight. Getting in the right frame of mind."

"Odets?"

"No. Peters—or is it Sklar? The first string critic gets Leo Murray's productions. All I get is W.P.A. shows and dramas of social significance. Which isn't so bad."

"I'll meet you at the hot-dog stand at 42nd and Broadway at eleven-thirty. It's a date."

He kissed her and started to leave.

"Don't forget," she called after him. "Master Charlie Beach might throw some stink bombs."

"Leo'll be lucky if he doesn't throw a stiletto."

At one o'clock, Leo Murray dismissed the company of *Hour's End*. Ricky Linton went out with Alice Lawrence. Bill Benedict met Leo and Boley in front of Sardi's.

The three of them made a quiet entrance into the restaurant. Boley and Bill led the way to a table. Leo followed, his dark eyes moving slowly over the faces around him. He went out of his way to nod to George S. Kaufman who was sitting alone looking like a weary, unshaven stumble-bum just off the rods.

They sat down. Leo called a waiter. "Bring some of that Lake trout for these boys. I'll take a double tomato juice."

"Maybe I don't like trout," Bill said.

"It's very good. You'll like it."

Bill sighed. He tore a roll in half and buttered it thickly. Boley winked to the waiter. "Bring me a big coke with the fish," he said. He winked again. The waiter went over to the bar.

"A coke for Frank Boley," the waiter told the barman. The barman nodded, dumped three fingers of Scotch in a coca-cola glass and diluted it with water.

"Nick Finley's just made an appearance," Bill said.

Leo's fingers tapped on the table. "Tell him to come over."

Bill rose and walked over to the cloakroom.

"Nick." A stocky man who looked more Jewish than the Irish he was, turned around.

"Hello, Bill."

"Leo wants to talk to you."

Nick felt in his breast pockets for his cigars. He took the hat-check from the girl and started toward an anteroom.

"Leo wants to see you, Nick."

"I don't play no command performances. Success hasn't turned Leo's head. He's still a louse."

Bill took Nick's arm. "Maybe you boys can get together for a good game of mumbly-peg."

Nick hesitated. He looked across the restaurant and saw Leo watching him, with a smile.

"Who's afraid?" Nick said. He followed Bill to the table.

"Hello, Leo."

"Hello, Nick. Sit down."

Finley kept his eyes on the top of Leo's head.

"Sit down, Nick. No one's going to bite."

The stocky Irishman sat down between Boley and Bill. He faced Leo. Leo called a waiter over. "An order of the trout for Mr. Finley."

"Make it a liver omelette, son," Nick said. "You should have been a nursemaid, Leo."

Leo grinned. "Or maybe a headwaiter."

"Got my show all set for tonight?" Nick said evenly.

Leo poured salt and pepper into his tomato juice. Boley was halfway through his second glass of spiked coke.

"Bill said you wanted to talk to me."

Leo wiped his hands on the napkin.

Nick Finley tapped his fingers on the table. "Suddenly get the guts to apologize for stealing my playwright?"

The tomato juice was being stirred. There was a long pause.

"You been talking around town that I stole *Hour's End* from you, Nicky," Leo said softly. "Don't you think it's god-damned unfriendly?"

"That's more truth than jingle."

Leo smiled without humor. "The truth is, Nick, that you'd still be peddling building supplies if it weren't for me."

Nick flushed. "You gave me a chance. So what?"

"So out of gratitude you stole the guy who put up money for my shows."

"Everything was above-board between us. You know that, Leo."

Nick's gold-rimmed glasses became misted. He wiped them.

"You double-crossed me on the Maxine Elliot Theater deal."

Nick was quiet.

"You tried to finagle a manager's contract with Alice Lawrence and you knew I wanted her. In short you been dedicating yourself to a life of knifing me. It probably flatters you. Reflected importance." Leo's voice grew louder. Everybody could hear him. "Nicky, you're only a road company edition of Leo Murray. You couldn't even get the first-string critics."

The Irishman's face filled with blood. He kept his glasses off and peered myopically at this little, proud dwarf. Slowly, he lowered his heavy lids and relaxed. He began to laugh loudly.

Finally, he spoke—a thin venom in his voice. "I'm just the Faust to your Mephisto, Leo. All I am, I owe to you. Does that salve you?"

"On second thought, Nick, you didn't steal my backer. He was merely looking for someone to get pretty actresses for him." Leo turned to Bill. "I hope you haven't forgotten to give Nick a couple of seats for the opening."

Finley rose abruptly, spilling some water on the table. He put his glasses on.

Leo turned to nod to an actress at another table.

"Some day, Leo," Nick said, "they're going to bury you. It'll be a nice day." He walked away from the table. Leo watched him go wistfully. He heard George Kaufman stage-whisper to a waiter. "I didn't know they had entertainment at Sardi's. Are those boys professionals or just underpaid hams?"

Leo's lips tightened. He looked at Boley. His business manager was finishing his third coke, unperturbed.

"Well?" Leo asked.

"It's none of my business," Bill said.

Leo laughed softly and finished his tomato juice. "Every man hates his master," he said, enjoying himself.

Boley laughed too loud. Bill kicked his foot under the table, but Boley kept on laughing.

"Shut up, Frank!" Leo was sore.

Frank covered his round, red face with a napkin and choked off the rest of the laugh.

Leo turned to Bill. "Find out any more about this Laney guy?"
"No."

"Are you sure someone sent him in to disrupt the show?"

"I could swear to it. Now, more than ever."

"Who do you think would do it?" Leo leaned back on his chair wearily.

Bill sipped some water. "You know who."

Leo scratched the tablecloth idly. Without looking at Bill, he said, "Finley?"

Bill nodded.

"What are we going to do about it?"

"We?" There was a sarcastic trace in Bill's tone.

"It's your job," Leo said curtly.

Bill shook his head slowly. "I'm no strong-arm man for you. I quit being that five years ago."

"You know, Bill . . ." Leo gazed off dreamily, "show business is overcrowded." He shrugged his thin shoulders. "And when you're overcrowded, what do you do?"

"You kill yourself," Bill said coldly.

Leo grinned. "I would. Only I'm too important."

CHAPTER IV
"CURTAIN GOING UP!"

It's a Broadway tradition that some producers never attend the opening nights of their shows. Some don't because they are afraid. Others, because they are not afraid but contemptuous. Leo was among these. He made an appointment to meet Bill Benedict at five-thirty at Bill's hotel, the Chicopee. At five-thirty he stepped into the Chicopee bar. Bill was waiting for him.

"I want your room for tonight," Leo said.

"Okay. Renovating your own place?"

"Too many people know my telephone number there. If Charlie Beach goes berserk, the papers'll be driving me nuts. I don't want to be bothered. You take care of them."

Bill picked an olive out of his Martini.

"Charlie Beach won't go near the theater."

"Did you see him?"

"No. I'm having a couple of cops around."

Leo looked worried. "That's not so good."

"It won't hurt the show."

"I'm not thinking of that." Leo lit a cigar. "Come back here when it's over."

"I got a date, Leo."

"It'll only take a minute. I want you back here. I want to hear about it."

"What'll I tell Charlie, if I see him?"

The producer ordered a beer. "Tell him if he breaks up my first night, I'll kill him."

"He'd love that. 'Producer Threatens Director, Beach Alleges.'"

"Tell him," said Leo, "I'll give him my next show to do."

"He'll believe you like Hitler."

Leo finished his drink. "Where are your keys?"

Bill gave them to him. Leo juggled them thoughtfully. "Don't forget to come right back. I'll be leaving here at eleven-thirty. You'll find your keys at the desk." He walked away.

Bill tried to get Sue on the phone. She wasn't at the office. He left word with the desk clerk to tell her when she came in that he was having dinner at Jack and Charlie's.

The restaurant was filled as usual with politicians, Yale, Harvard and Princeton cut-purses, and those whose lives are bounded on the north by 52nd Street and on the south by Winchell's column.

Bill said hello to Henry and Katherine Traube, and joined them at their table. "How's the law, Hank?"

"An assistant D.A. for a husband," Katherine said, "is like sleeping with nine old men. It's no fun kissing a misdemeanor."

"I prefer a tort, myself," Bill said.

"You know Nick Finley, don't you, Bill?" Henry asked.

"Sure."

"Nice guy?"

"Some people prefer the movies."

"He came in the office this afternoon."

Bill looked up with interest. "The D.A.'s office?"

"Yes."

"Complaining about a garbage ordinance?"

"Wants a warrant charging defamation of character against Leo Murray."

"Has he got a witness?"

"Sardi's Restaurant, West 44th Street, between the hours of one-thirty and two, October 22, 1938."

"That's a lot of witness."

A taxicab drew up at the corner of 65th and Lexington Avenue. Ricky Linton and Alice Lawrence got out. Ricky paid the cabdriver, and remained standing at the corner with Alice until he drove away.

"We've got to call him first," Alice said unsteadily.

Ricky looked at his wristwatch. "Six-thirty."

"He may be home."

"There's a drugstore at the corner. We'll call from there."

They started to walk toward it. Alice was dressed in a long, flowing evening outfit; Ricky wore tails. Both had been drinking.

"What'll you say if he answers the phone?"

Ricky struck a lighter nervously. He grinned sardonically. "I'll wish him luck."

In front of the drugstore Ricky looked at his watch again. "You better come inside with me, Alice. Somebody may pass by and see you."

"God, I hate this," she said.

He turned to her sharply. "It was your idea."

"I know." She gave him a swift, bright smile. "No falling out for these thieves, darling."

He pressed her fingers. "You don't get rid of a rat by moral persuasion."

They entered the store. While Alice was buying a magazine and cigarettes, Ricky stepped back into the store to the telephone booth. He dialed a number, listened to the long and short buzzes, and finally hung up.

"Paid for the magazine, dear?" he asked when he came up to Alice.

She nodded.

"We ought to be going now."

They headed for a small apartment house. "He wasn't in," Ricky said.

"What about Ruth?"

"I spoke to her earlier. She said she was hanging around the office until show time." Ricky kept pressing his lighter and blowing the flame out.

"That's a bad habit, Ricky."

He stuck the lighter back in his vest pocket. They came up to a small apartment house.

"Here it is." They looked up and down the street before entering. The lobby was empty.

"Self-running elevator," Alice murmured.

"That helps."

They went up to the fourth floor. Ricky took a master key out of his pocket. The door opened easily. Ricky closed it quietly behind them.

"Where's the desk, Alice? You've been here before." He was grinning maliciously.

"Ricky! Stop it!"

"Sorry."

He twirled his lighter. "It doesn't give much light."

Alice walked over to a closet and snapped a switch.

"That's better. Where's the desk?"

Alice pointed to a large Jacobean desk. "If I open the closet door wider, you can see better."

Ricky tried all the drawers. They were unlocked. Quickly he took all the papers out of them and passed some to Alice.

"Look through these."

Ricky filled his hands with papers and sat on the floor near the closet. "He's got more junk in here than the World's Fair."

Alice sighed nervously. "The desk alone'll take us more than an hour."

"It has to be done."

"What if we don't find them? What'll we do?"

Ricky fingered the papers.

"What'll we do?"

Ricky kept his eyes away from Alice.

By eight-fifteen the lobby of the Arcadia was crowded. The first-nighters eddied around the ticket entrance where Jimmy Burke in a tuxedo snapped their paste boards and passed the customers inside. Sentineal, the doorman, opened limousine doors with an Edwardian dignity and offered his hand to various dowagers. On the sidewalks loitered the critics. Brooks Atkinson of the *Times*, nervous and scholarly, greeted Heywood Broun. The fat Voltaire was shabbily dressed as ever.

Bill arrived with the Traubes. It bothered him that it was close to eight-thirty. He checked up with Jimmy Burke.

"Seen Charlie Beach around?"

"I've been too busy to watch, Bill. But what about this Laney guy?"

"He won't show up. He's allergic to cops."

On the sidewalk, there was a little flurry. Frederick MacMonnies was being congratulated. He was with a tall, exotic, blond woman.

Bill went backstage.

"Charlie Beach?" he asked Steve.

"Look in the prop room, Bill. Last time I seen him he was fitting on a mask to frighten Leo with."

"Go to hell and good luck."

Bill hung around outside mingling with the crowds. At eight-thirty, Sentineal told him that Steve Levy wanted to see him. They met at the stage door. Steve was nervous.

"We've called ten minutes. Lawrence isn't here yet."

"Is she on at the opening?"

"About ten speeches after." Steve wiped his grimy face. "What the hell we gonna do?"

A taxi jogged to a halt in front of them. Ricky Linton in tails and Alice Lawrence in evening clothes stepped out.

"You're late," snapped Bill.

"Go to hell, darling. I've never been late to my openings."

"Where's Leo?" Ricky asked.

Bill walked away. Ricky pulled him back.

"Where's Leo?"

"At night school."

"It's important. I want to see him."

"Get into your make-up, Alice," Bill said.

Ricky took the actress's arm and entered the stage door with her.

"I'd like to kick his pants off," Steve said.

"He owns fifty per cent of the show," Bill said. "Try it next year."

Steve moved his hands in resignation. "I've taken castor-oil. I can take Linton."

Sentineal and Jimmy Burke were chanting: "Curtain going . . . up! Curtain going . . . up! Curtain going . . . up!"

Steve went backstage. Bill remained out front.

At eight forty-five, he took one last look around and entered the theater. "If Charlie tries to come in," he told Jimmy Burke, "I'll be at the end of the middle aisle, standing."

The house lights dimmed. Bill loved this moment in the theater; that split-second expectation when the footlights from the apron threw a rich yellow spread up on the curtain. The audience fell into a sudden, irretrievable hush. . . . The curtain rose . . . slowly.

Bill knew the play by heart. He spent the first act scanning the audience looking for Beach. By the second-act intermission he knew that *Hour's End* was in the bag. He could tell by the sour expression on George Jean Nathan's face and the beaming blush on the New York *Times'* Atkinson. In the lobby, Nick Finley was looking like an orphan of the storm. Bill went over.

"Don't look so sour, Nicky."

"Sour? A half a million bucks this show'll make. You like to get gypped out of a fortune?"

"Next time."

"Leo's a four star crook. You can wire that for sound."

"What the hell? Dog eat dog. It's show business."

"I know one dog who ought to be spayed."

Bill smiled. "You'll feel better tomorrow." He left Nick. Jimmy Burke was calling, "Curtain."

"Where's Ruth Murray?" Bill asked.

"Sitting in J 106."

"Thanks." He re-entered the theater. When the stage lights came on he looked for J 106. He saw her, hunched forward, intent on the stage.

Near the middle of the last act, Jimmy Burke went over to Bill. and whispered, "Charlie Beach. Sneaked in through a fire door."

Bill turned swiftly. "Where is he?"

"Standing near the last aisle."

Bill moved toward him. Charlie was gripping the railing, his eyes shining with the reflected stage light. Bill took his arm. Charlie turned wildly.

"Lemme alone."

"Shut up. There's a show going on."

People turned in their seats and began to "shush." Charlie quieted down.

"Outside with me," Bill said.

"Let me stay."

"You'll raise a stink."

"I won't."

"Then come outside."

"I want to see what he did to it. I want to see how he used my stuff." Charlie's voice grew louder. An usher came over.

Bill pulled him away from the rail. With his fist muffled by a glove he hit Charlie across the jaw. He stripped the glove off quickly and stuffed it in Charlie's mouth. Jimmy Burke helped him take the boy through the box-office door. Frank Boley was counting up.

"He'll come to in a minute," Bill said.

"You hit him hard."

"Frank, douse that on him. I caught him before he had a chance to yell."

Frank swished an open bottle of coca-cola smelling of Scotch on Charlie's pale face. His eyes opened. He looked at Bill ruefully.

"You didn't have to do it."

"Sorry, kid."

"Call a cop?" Jimmy Burke asked.

Charlie's eyes clouded with terror. "No cops, Bill."

"Forget it," Boley said.

Bill thought for a moment. "Okay. If I see you back in the theater, it'll be cops and worse."

"Where's Leo?" Charlie asked huskily.

Bill walked out without answering.

The play had progressed to the point where Alice Lawrence was to speak the lines which she and Leo had argued about that afternoon.

The actress hesitated. She looked up at a box where Leo might have been sitting. Then, slowly, with careful emphasis she read them *as she wanted them.*

Bill waited to see whether Steve would lower the curtain as per Leo's orders. It remained aloft. Bill sighed and left the theater.

He walked back to the Chicopee. He squinted in his mail box for messages. He took the elevator up to the fourth floor. His door was unlocked and the room was dark. He stepped forward to the switch. As he reached out, something crashed down on his head. He fell to the floor, unconscious.

CHAPTER V
OPENING NIGHT PARTY

At the hot-dog stand, Sue Huxley waited for Bill until midnight. She called him all the names in the Schimpflexicon and walked to the Chicopee.

"Is Mr. Benedict in?" she asked the desk clerk.

He looked warily at her, then looked away. "I didn't see him."

"Call him on the phone."

The clerk did.

There was no answer.

Sue muttered something about men being punks and asked for her room-key.

When she got in the elevator, the boy told her that he had taken Bill up an hour ago. She got out on the fourth floor. Bill's door was open. She walked in, turned up the light and screamed. Bill was lying at her feet with blood on his head. . . . Near him was Leo Murray. A long hunting knife stood upright in his back. Sue forgot to scream and fell to her knees beside Bill. She tried to pick him up. He groaned. "Bill. . . . Bill, darling. Are you all right, honey?"

He groaned some more and got up to his hands and knees.

"Bill . . . are you hurt?"

He rubbed his temple and looked at the blood on his hands. "Sue, why did you do it?" he demanded angrily. "It's a helluva trick to play on a guy!"

"Bill!"

He looked where she was pointing. He blinked drunkenly. Then his vision cleared. "Jesus!" He felt Leo's head. The man was dead.

"Were you here when it happened?" Sue was almost in tears.

Bill didn't answer. He was still looking at the body. It was flat on its face. The knife, six inches below the collar. Blood dripped from the coat.

"Poor guy's dead," he muttered huskily. He shook his head unbelieving.

Sue moved close to Leo.

"Don't touch it!"

"He's dead! Leo Murray's dead! Oh my God, where's your phone?"

Bill caught her arm. "Forget you're a reporter for a minute, will you? Leo Murray was murdered in my apartment. With my hunting knife. What does that make me?"

Sue dropped the phone.

"The murderer?"

"Yeah. . . . It's the perfect conclusion."

Sue picked up the phone again. "I better call the house dick."

"No."

"What then?"

"This isn't what I'd call a soft spot." The two of them looked at each other solemnly. Then Bill touched Sue's hand. "Don't worry, kid. Not too much."

He crossed to the windows and lowered the shades. He looked in the bathroom and kitchen.

"For God's sake, don't look for clues, Bill. This isn't the time for an ex-detective."

"And it isn't something you get in a lending library for three cents a day."

Sue sat down gingerly. "I don't have to say I found you here. . . . I've got some money you can borrow."

"I'm not running out."

"Let me call the house dick," Sue pleaded. "Help me wash this blood off my face."

She got a wet towel.

"Be careful, Sue."

"Maybe this will turn out to be just the second feature on a double bill," she said dabbing at his face carefully.

"The murderer was here when I came in."

"Maybe he's still here."

"No."

"How do you know?"

"I just looked through the place."

"You can't tell a fingerprint from a horseshoe. For the third time, let me call the house dick."

Bill folded the towel abstractedly. He put it back in the bathroom.

"It's a pretty bit of evidence you're hanging in there."

Bill put on his topcoat.

"Bill . . ."

"If you mention that house dick again . . ."

"I'm worried."

"Get your duds."

"Where we going?"

Bill helped her on with the coat. He turned oft the lights in the room, locked the door behind them, and rang for an elevator.

Downstairs, the desk clerk took a look at the egg-sized swelling over Bill's right eye, and smirked. "Did you fall, Mr. Benedict?"

"A mosquito bite," Sue said, trying to keep a tremor out of her voice.

"Harry. Anybody go up to my room tonight between ten and eleven?"

Harry thought for a minute and fiddled with the desk pen. "No, Mr. Benedict. I didn't even see you go up. Miss Huxley asked for you and I told her you were out."

"Thanks."

Bill waited until the three elevator boys were on the main floor. He collected them together.

"You boys take anybody up to 412 between ten and eleven?"

"Lots to the fourth floor," Redhead replied.

"To 412?"

Two of them shook their heads. Redhead said: "Lots don't mention the room number."

"Did you take anybody up to any floor who was a friend of mine or . . . Leo Murray's?"

"Lots," said Redhead.

"Kid, you've seen too many movies. . . . Let's go, Sue."

On the sidewalk outside the hotel, Bill hesitated a minute, lit a cigarette; then started for the Arcadia Theater.

"You ought to call the cops, now," Sue said disconsolately.

He didn't reply.

"The cops don't like people who don't tell them about a murder. It says so in the telephone book. 'I want a policeman.'" Sue put her hand in his pocket and clasped his fingers. "I'm terribly worried, Bill."

Bill saw Frank Boley ahead of them, rocking like a coal barge in a cross sea. "What's an hour in the life of a cop? Let's go over and talk to Frank."

"Bill. . . . Bill. . . . Bill. . . . H'ya, Bill!"

"Boley, you're tanked up," Bill said.

"Come . . . boys and girls. A drink." Boley put his arm around Sue. "You're an . . . okay lass."

"Where's Leo?" Bill was impatient.

"Hurray for Leo . . . Got a hit . . . Man of hits." He belched. "Pardon. Belchin's good for the soul."

"Where's Leo?"

"Whaddya wanna know for?"

"Got a hundred grand movie offer for *Hour's End*."

"Thas important, Bill. Very important, Bill. Gotta get to Leo right away." He staggered over to a wall and supported himself. "Leo very funny guy. Opening night. No one knows where he keeps himself. Don't want to see nobody. . . . Well, that's where he is now. . . ."

"Where?"

"Where no one can see him."

"Where the hell is that, Frank?"

Boley took a long breath and squinted his eyes to get a better look at Sue. "Where no one can see him. The hell with Leo and the hundred grand. Let's all go for a drink."

"Thanks," said Bill, starting to walk away.

"Wait a minute!" Boley grabbed Bill's arm. He fumbled in his pockets. Finally, he took out an envelope and handed it to Bill.

"When you see Leo . . . give 'im this message. It's somethin' he left in the box office for MacMonnies. Mac read it and wrote an answer in it. . . . Crazy business. . . . Comin' for a drink?"

"Tomorrow night, Frank."

Bill walked away with Sue. "Boley was stinko," she said.

"Yeah . . . I've never seen him that drunk before."

"Maybe he was putting on an act."

Bill laughed shortly. "If he was, he's a better actor than all the Barrymores rolled into Charlie McCarthy."

They found Steve Levy at the theater. He was sitting in one of the dressing rooms, haggard and dirty, having coffee out of a container with his wife. Introductions were made back and forth.

"Forget something, Bill?" Steve asked.

"I want to check up for Leo. What time did the curtain fall at the end of the show?"

Steve took a piece of grimy paper out of his back-pocket and referred to it. "Eleven-two."

"Was everybody on stage for it?"

Steve grinned. "Who'd miss a curtain call? There isn't an actor born—"

"Are you sure?"

"Yes. . . ." Steve looked queerly at Bill. "Why?"

"Ricky Linton?"

"Yes. . . ."

"Did MacMonnies take a bow?"

"No. A bunch of his friends yelled, 'author' but he wasn't around. I looked for him. Why the inquisition?"

Sue spoke quickly. "Leo Murray's dead."

Steve paled. "You're kidding."

"Sure, she's kidding," said Bill, pinching Sue's arm.

"Ouch!"

"That, my darling, is for letting wish-fulfillment get the better of you. Good night, Steve and Mrs. Steve. See you tomorrow."

He pushed Sue ahead of him and went out the stage door. "I'll break your sweet little neck if you double-cross me," Bill said angrily. Sue mumbled something, and they got into a cab.

"Where we heading for now, Bill?"

"To the home of the missing author, Mister Frederick Mac-Monnies. He didn't wait to take a bow. For a playwright, that's damned suspicious."

MacMonnies lived in one of those equivocal apartment houses in the West Seventies where opera singers, photographers, and expensive ladies have their studios. There was a little lobby downstairs and no elevator. Bill rang the downstairs bell under Mac's name. He lived two flights up. As they approached the door of his apartment, they heard the thick drumming of some unfamiliar music coming from it. Bill looked around for a bell. He couldn't find one. He knocked. No one answered.

"Maybe he's asleep," Sue suggested.

"That music you hear is no snore."

Bill knocked again. "I know there's someone in there," he said. "I'll kick the blasted door down before I give up."

He knocked the third time. Someone fumbled with a chain. In a crack of the door MacMonnies squinted at them.

"What do you want?"

A scent seeped through the open door from the room. Not quite Oriental. More like a cavern—mossy smell.

"Can we come in for a minute? This is Miss Huxley, Mr. Mac-Monnies."

MacMonnies turned his head and muttered a couple of words to someone inside. Finally, he opened the door.

The apartment was dark. The few lights were covered with a red paint. There was an illuminated statue in a corner. Before Bill had a chance to get a closer look someone turned off the light. The room was even darker. There were other men and women present.

"What do you want?"

"How about a little light?" Bill said, feeling Sue step closer to him.

"I didn't ask you to come," Mac said coldly.

The drumming music got louder. It came from a huge Capehart in a far corner of the room.

"I can't talk with that sounding off. Let's step out in the hallway."

A tall, heavily made-up blond woman came over and smiled. Bill nodded. He had seen her at the show with MacMonnies.

Mac grumbled an introduction. Her name was Madame Kyra. She opened the door. The four of them stepped out into the hallway.

"You're a hospitable guy, Mac."

The playwright started to re-enter his apartment.

"Wait a minute." Bill caught his arm. Mac shook free instantly and faced him. "There's something else. Did you see the final curtain of your show tonight?"

"Are you investigating for the Watch and Ward Society?" Mac was a little tight.

"Leo was murdered about that time."

"Too bad."

"He wasn't at the theater."

"I didn't look for him."

"No one but me knew where he was." Mac kept buttoning and unbuttoning his coat. "But maybe I'm wrong. Did you know where he was?"

The playwright opened his eyes a trifle. "No."

"You're a liar." Bill handed him the note he got from Boley. Mac read it and tore it up.

"Still a liar," Bill said dogmatically.

Mac tightened up a little and swung his left hand at Bill. Bill tried to duck. He was too slow. Mac's fist caught his jaw. He fell to the floor. Sue screamed. Mac went back into his apartment and locked the door.

Sue helped Bill up.

"That's sock number two for you tonight," she murmured.

Bill remained for a moment in front of MacMonnies' door. The music coming through sounded like the wail of a manic-depressive taking the water cure.

"Let's go, Bill," Sue pleaded.

Reflectively he rubbed the place where Mac had hit him. "I could knock that door in."

Sue stepped in front of him. "Please don't."

Bill thought a minute. Sue pushed him to the stairway.

"Don't be crazier than you have to be, Bill. There's no point to it. Let's call the cops and go back to the hotel. You're making trouble for yourself. You're no licensed detective any more. Just an ordinary citizen." She held his arm pleadingly. "If you don't do what I tell you, I'm going to call the cops myself."

Bill took a dime out of his pocket and prepared to flip it. "Heads we break in, tails we go back to the hotel." He flipped the dime. It was tails.

CHAPTER VI
ENTER: MR. POTTS

"What made him sock you?" Sue asked in the cab.

"Crime reporters call it 'consciousness of guilt.'"

"That's a hasty conclusion, Mr. Vance."

Sue looked up at Bill. He bent over and kissed her.

"This is no time for sentiment," she said.

"Every great detective needs a little needling once in a while." Bill put his arm around her and pulled her close to him.

"What made him sock you?"

Bill was staring out of the window. "It'll help a lot if MacMonnies turned up to be the guilty party of the first part."

"It's not possible."

"Why not?"

"Didn't you ever read detective stories, Mr. Benedict?"

"Sure. From Anna Katherine Green through Ellery Queen to Marco Page." He flipped his cigarette out of the window. "What about it?"

"The first person suspected is never guilty." She patted his arm smugly.

"You're a mote in the eye of progress. Have you forgotten that I'm the first suspect?"

At the Chicopee, the desk clerk stepped out to meet Bill at the elevator. "There's someone up in your room to see you, Mr. Benedict."

"It isn't by any chance a sourpuss in a shiny serge suit?"

"No, Mr. Benedict. The man is wearing a loud check."

"A detective," Bill said.

The clerk walked away.

"I'm getting cold feet, Bill," Sue said in the elevator.

"Keep your lips well rouged and stick as close as you can to the truth." He turned to the elevator boy. "I ask her and she won't marry me."

"I don't blame her. . . . Fourth floor," Redhead replied.

Bill and Sue walked into the large, checkered and capacious arms of Detective-Lieutenant Potts, one of the more capable instruments of the law. Hake Potts was almost as broad as he was tall, meaning that he was built like a six-foot length of water conduit. He had been in charge of the Broadway district from the ingénue days of Ethel Barrymore. He knew everybody and distrusted everybody, which made him very efficient.

"Hello, Benedict," he said. "Don't you know the criminal never returns to the scene of his crime?" He doffed his cap to Sue. "Miss Huxley of the *Examiner* drammer page. Looks as if I walked right into a rehearsal."

Bill was looking for Murray's body.

"Leo has an aisle seat in the morgue. Don't bother looking for him." He moved a couple of chairs together. "Sit down, my friends, and tell Potts all about it."

Bill glanced at the blood stains on the floor, then sank into the chair. He nodded to Sue. She sat down, too. Bill suddenly leaned forward toward the detective.

"What time did you get here?"

Potts slid a cuff back and looked at his wristwatch. "An hour and a half ago. Twelve-fifteen."

"Who told you to come?"

Potts grinned and said mildly, "How about you bein' on the receiving end for a while?" Bill chuckled. "Thanks. What was Murray doing here tonight?"

"I lent him my place. His show was opening—"

"*Hour's End*, wasn't it?"

"Yes. He didn't want to be bothered at his home. I came back here at about eleven o'clock. I walked in; the room was dark; I go to turn up a light; I get knocked out."

"Sounds like The March of Time," Potts said. "How come ya wasn't here when *I* walked in."

"Miss Huxley found me. We went out for a bite to eat."

"Maybe you thought Murray was on the floor looking for termites."

Bill lit a cigarette. "I knew he was dead."

"Whyn't ya call the police department?" Potts took a package of chewing gum out of his pocket and split the cellophane angrily. "Whyn't ya?" He threw three chiclets into his mouth. "The last time ya got into trouble I took your dick's license away from ya. This time, I'll put ya away for good."

"See . . ." Sue said.

"Don't lay it on," Bill said. He arose and walked around the room. Potts followed him with his large, Irish setter eyes.

"It didn't look too good for me," Bill said, finally. "I played a hunch. I thought I'd find something to clear me before the cops stepped in."

"And messed things up, eh? You think cops are pretty dumb about these things, don'cha? You was going to have the case all cracked. All we gotta do is to make the arrest. You think the boys in blue are on the dumb-wit side." He blew the gum into his palm and threw it in a wastepaper basket angrily. "That's what comes of readin' all them screwy detective stories."

"He's sorry," Sue said.

"What was your hunch?" Potts asked.

"That there were others besides me who knew where Leo Murray was staying."

"Not a bad hunch," Potts said grudgingly. "Who?"

"Frederick MacMonnies. I'll give you his address. Author of *Hour's End*. He knew."

"How?" The detective put some more gum in his mouth.

"Boley, Leo's business manager met us at 45th Street when we left here. He gave me a note. Leo had left it in the box-office for MacMonnies. Boley gave it to Mac who read it and put it back. The note asked Mac to call Leo at my room during the first intermission."

"So that's why he socked you," Sue said sagely.

"I went up to Mac's place. We chatted a bit, then he socked me with a tire iron."

"His fist, darling. I saw it coming."

"I read the note before I gave it to Mac."

"How do you know," asked Potts moving his jaws slowly, "that MacMonnies saw the note before you gave it to him?"

"Boley told me. Mac saw it and told Boley to give it back to Leo with some unladylike comments."

"Fits."

"More than that. Let MacMonnies prove he was in the theater during the last act. If he can't maybe that means he dashed over here a little before eleven and laid Leo out. I place the murder about that time."

Potts nodded.

"And that, Mr. Lieutenant, comes from reading those screwy detective stories."

Sue was beaming. Potts crunched his gum noisily.

"Where's the note?" Potts asked, after a while.

"Mac tore it up."

"So. . . ."

"What about it?"

"You and MacMonnies are the only ones who knew where Murray was."

"Boley knew if he read the note."

"By your own story, the note's the only thing that implicated MacMonnies. That right?"

Bill took a deep breath. "Yes."

"And according to that story there ain't no more note. Did you bring the pieces with you?"

"No."

"So all I got's your word."

"Not everybody has my word."

Potts concentrated his big eyes on an imaginary object on the ceiling. "Did you see the knife that killed Murray?"

Bill hesitated. "Yes."

"Recognize it?" Potts jaws moved faster.

"Yes. It's mine."

"What are you doing with a hunting knife in the middle of Broadway?"

Sue laughed nervously. "Ol' Daniel Benedict, the Times Square trapper."

"It was given to me."

"Boy Scouts?"

"Fine Steel Company of New Haven. I was doing some promotion for them."

"You know what I think?" Potts asked mildly.

"What?"

"That you're a liar." He rose and yawned. "And I'm too tired to find out why. So instead of crawling between two cool hotel sheets, you come along with me and try a night at the station-house." He moved his two-hundred pounds of pavement-pounder to the door and sighed. "Tomorrow is another day. Everything's always different tomorrow. Like day from night."

"Don't worry, darling," said Sue, close to tears. "I'll give you the best death-house interview in the history of journalism."

"That's a lousy joke," Bill said. And kissed her.

The next morning, about ten o'clock, Hake Potts opened the door of Bill's cell.

"Come out and have some breakfast," he said in a friendly way. He took Bill into his office and handed him a morning paper.

A waiter entered with a tray of food.

"Feed all your prisoners this way?" Bill asked.

Potts shook his head. "Extra-official."

"What makes me so goddamned important?"

"A fellow talks better on a full stomach." Potts leaned over the table heavily and emerged with a roll which he proceeded to plaster with butter and jelly.

"Reducing?" asked Bill.

"No. Takes a lot of them vitamins to keep me going. Three thousand a day. I count 'em."

Bill dug into a grapefruit.

"Whyn't you tell me about Charlie Beach last night?"

Bill looked up and wiped his mouth slowly. "How did you find out about Charlie?"

"You asked the cops to watch for him at the Arcadia last night. Why'nt you tell me?"

Bill concentrated on the food.

"I'm waiting to hear."

Bill remained silent.

"Need an earphone, Mr. Benedict?"

"Listen, Mr. Detective. When I'm finished with breakfast, you're either going to let me go or charge me with something so I can get a lawyer. Either way, I'm as dumb as Harpo Marx."

Potts looked at him, amazed. "Now, that's not what I call the co-operative spirit."

"Hell, *you* arrested me."

"I didn't arrest ya. I took ya here to spend the night with us."

"Then give me my money back. The place stinks. And if your charge doesn't hold water, I'm going to sue the city."

Potts poured some coffee into Bill's cup. "Sugar?"

Bill laughed. "Two. And cream." He watched Potts' thick fingers drop the pieces in. He laughed again. "Butler service at a police station. No one would believe it."

"I found out a lot of things this morning I didn't know last night," Potts said ingratiatingly.

"I'm not interested."

Potts buttered another piece of roll. "Sometimes a guy can't help being interested."

Bill put his coffee down. "What do you mean?"

A sergeant in uniform entered and gave Potts a note. The detective read it and his face reddened.

He finished his toast in silence.

"Got a cigarette, Mr. Potts?"

Potts took out a pack. "Benedict, I think we was all carried away last night by what I call the trim of the situation. The gadgets, the chromium buttons that don't mean nothing. There's gotta be a slight change in schedule."

Bill blew out some smoke. "If you're laying on the soft soap, Mr. Potts, thinking you're going to get me to break down and confess, you're as wrong as Hitler."

"No soft soap, Benedict. For the electric chair, you're a little ahead of time."

Bill rose. "Fine. That leaves me this morning free to get a lawyer to draw up a bill of complaint against the city."

"You can't go yet. I just got a report from the Medical Examiner."

"I suppose they found my fingerprints on the knife," Bill said bitterly. "*My* knife. Why shouldn't they?"

"Don't worry about fingerprints. The knife was as clean as the Legion of Decency. For me, it's worse than that. Ya said ya came into your hotel room at about eleven?"

"Yes."

Potts tossed some gum into his mouth. His big eyes were sad. "That's too bad. . . . Ya see the Medical Examiner says Murray was killed between the hours of eight and eight-thirty."

Bill smiled broadly.

"That sorta opens the field wide. It cuts ya off the list of suspects."

"That's tough for you."

"Worse." Potts chewed glumly. "You got a perfect alibi."

"Who?"

"By sheer accident you was having something to eat with Assistant District Attorney Traube at that time."

"How do you know?"

"He's in charge of the Murray case. He told me early this morning. It was no alibi then." He pointed to the Medical Examiner's report. "It is now."

"Have some coffee, Lieutenant? Sugar?"

"Go to hell."

"Anything else?"

Potts scrounged uncomfortably in his chair. "I'm no heel, Benedict."

"Okay."

"A guy can make mistakes." The jaws had a dirge-like rhythm.

"Sure."

"Then, let bygones be bygones. . . . I need some help."

"What'll you give me?"

"Your detective agency license back."

"What do you want?"

"Draw me up a list of everybody you know who had a grudge against Murray?"

"That's easy," said Bill. "It's all done."

"Where?"

"Who's Who in the American Theater."

Potts sighed like a tree falling. "Offhand," he said, "I'd be sore at a wisecrack like that." Suddenly, he frowned. "Bill, you're going to help me whether ya like it or not."

"Well. . . . If you ask me that way."

"I'm not asking no more. I'm telling ya. For your own health. There was two people that come in to your room last night. The guy who bumped off Leo, and the guy who socked you."

"Why can't they be the same?"

Potts spit out his gum in disgust. "No murderer waits around for three hours just to bang a book-end on your head."

Bill stared away abstractedly. "All right, there were two."

"The second guy can't be sure whether ya got anything on him. Maybe ya recognized him as he swung at ya. Maybe ya caught a glimpse when ya fell. He can't be sure. That means he's gonna get after ya to find out how much ya know. If he thinks ya know too much—" Potts left the sentence in mid-air.

Bill's eyes narrowed. He wiped his lips with a napkin and took a deep puff of his cigarette. He squashed it.

"I'm not frightened, but I'll help."

"Swell." Potts stuck out a hand. "And ya can go back and become a private dick all over again."

"I'm going to sue the city anyway."

Potts lumbered over to him. "Sue and be damned. This is Broadway. I need the help of a Broadway in-and-outer. . . . See that the *Hour's End* company remains on stage after the performance tonight. I want to see them actors and actresses. Sometimes ya turn over a stone and you find a black widow spider. I gotta find out who could've been free at eight."

"Placing the murder at that time doesn't help. Broadway's a big place."

Potts pulled at his knuckles. "Christ, I can't exx everybody in the theatrical business."

"Sure." Bill started for the door and stopped. "Lieutenant, I got one question to ask you."

"We're buddies. Go ahead." Potts was looking longingly at the remnants of the breakfast.

"Who told you to come up to my room last night?"

"A call came in about midnight."

"Man or woman?"

"Man. We checked the call. It came from a pay station at a drugstore on 45th Street."

"Midnight at 45th Street." It seemed as if Bill were memorizing the phrase.

"Why?"

"You can reach me at Murray's office. I'll be there all day," Bill said, and left.

Bill had a shower and took a cab to the Regent Theater Building. There was a little knot of reporters in the lobby downstairs.

"What's the good news, Bill?" The man from the *Sun* asked.

"Is it true that Leo killed himself to get even with the critics?"

"He was the victim of a creeping ego."

"A peeping Tom."

Bill stopped the chaff and said, "He's dead. You can quote me on that."

"What was he doing up in your room?"

"How come Huxley of the *Examiner* got in first with the story?"

Bill said, stepping into the elevator. "On second thought, you better not quote me."

"We're sure gonna miss Mister Murray," Angus said. The tall, good-looking Negro who had seen them come and go, the friend and confidant of every Broadwayite from Dan Frohman to Detective-Lieutenant Potts, was sad.

"Angus, I bet you're one of the select few who'll really mourn."

Bill entered the office. Ruth Murray was hunched up at a desk, her eyes red-rimmed with weeping, her hair askew, with no make-up on. Like an automaton she sat there cutting the reviews from the morning papers just as she had done on the mornings after all of Leo's shows.

"Come over, Bill," she said in a low, dead voice. She rose from her stenographer's chair and walked to the window. "I feel so terrible, Bill." The words came hoarsely out of a genuine grief. He put his hand on Ruth's shoulder.

"Go home, Ruth. It's better at home."

"Who could've done such a thing?" She pressed her lips together in pain.

"Why don't you take the day off, Ruth? We can run the office without you."

She looked away. "No. There's a lot to do today. You know what it is. The first day after an opening."

"When's the funeral going to be?"

"This afternoon."

"Need any ready cash?"

She shook her head and sat down at the desk. "Leo would have loved to see how fine the critics were to his play."

"Yeah. . . ."

Ruth pressed her hand across her eyes. Her voice was low.

"There are so many things I want to say about him." She fumbled with a pair of scissors. "People only knew the side of him that . . . that was rotten."

"We're all rotten at times, Ruth." Bill was silent for a moment. "Leo never got married, did he?"

Ruth cut into a clipping. "Not that I know of."

"That means . . . everything'll go to you."

She said solemnly, "I don't know . . . I really don't care. I wish he was still alive. That's all I wish."

Bill patted her arm gently. "I'll be in my office, if you want anything."

Bill walked down the hall. He saw Boley's red face as he entered the business manager's office.

"Good morning, Frank."

Boley sat at his desk like a man in a cataleptic trance.

"I want to talk to you, Frank."

"Get the hell out of here," Boley cried. "I don't want to talk to no one."

Bill snapped a match across his nail and blew it out after a while.

"Okay."

He found Ricky Linton and Steve in his own office.

Ricky was sitting on the desk swinging his long legs. "God's gift to the American Theater got his," Ricky chirped.

"Cut it out!" said Bill.

"De mortuis nil nisi bonum, eh?"

"Oh for Christ sake, Linton," Steve burst out.

The telephone rang. It was Ruth.

"Lieutenant Potts to see you."

"Tell him to come in."

Potts entered with Ruth and Boley. Bill introduced him to Linton and Steve. Potts was still wearing his checked serge suit. It made him look a little on the burlesque comedian side.

He sat down at Bill's desk, drew a pad out of his pocket and a pencil.

"I've got a simple question I wanna ask all of you."

Ricky murmured: "Looks like I've seen this picture before."

"Miss Murray," Potts said. "Where were you last night at eight o'clock?"

Ruth spoke quietly. "I was at the office. My brother called me about six to tell me to wait for him there. At eight, he didn't show up. I thought he changed his mind. A little after eight I left and had a bite to eat in Childs."

"What Childs?"

"Paramount Building."

"Did you see anybody you know there?"

"No. Angus, the elevator boy, took me down when I left the office."

Potts made a note. "Did your brother tell you where he was?"

"No. If he had I would have called him to find out why he hadn't come back here."

"All right, Miss Murray. Thanks. You can go now."

Ruth hesitated a moment. Then she looked at each of the men in the room with her wide, grieved eyes, and went out.

A heavy, empty silence. Potts coughed and shoved his heavy body around to face Linton.

"You, Mr. Linton. Where were you at eight last night?"

"You ought to get someone to write your dialogue for you, Lieutenant. I've heard that line before."

"Shut up and answer my question."

"You see—that's just what I mean."

Potts chewed violently without speaking.

"I was in a taxicab from eight to eight-thirty." Linton smiled.

"Where'd you get on?"

"Sheridan Square. And I got off at the Arcadia Theater. And it doesn't take a half hour to make the trip is what you're thinking. But you're wrong."

"I'll make up my own mind about that. What company cab?"

Linton tapped a cigarette on his thumbnail. "Terminal."

Potts jotted it down. "Do you know Charlie Beach?"

Linton's eyes widened. "Yes."

"When was the last time you seen him?"

"I . . . I don't remember."

"Did you know where Murray was last night?"

"No."

"Okay. You can beat it now." Potts turned to Steve. "What's on your mind, Mr. Levy?"

"I was at the theater from seven-thirty until eleven-thirty." Linton was listening carefully.

"Do you keep a record of stage-hands and the cast, Mr. Levy?"

"Not exactly a written record."

"Anybody come in late—after eight?"

Steve thought a moment, avoiding Linton's stare. "Alice Lawrence."

"When she come in?"

"At eight-thirty . . . with Mr. Linton."

"In a cab?"

"Yes."

"What kind?"

Linton interrupted. "The reason Miss Lawrence was late was because she wasn't feeling well. I called for her at her apartment at seven-thirty. We were together from that time on."

Potts passed a box of chiclets around. He yawned and scratched the pad with his pencil. "I suppose Miss Lawrence will say she was with you at that time, eh? That gives you both an alibi."

Ricky nodded patly.

"Reminds me of the time Granville Barker was robbed by two hoofers. The boys alibied each other." He chuckled. "Both of 'em was guilty."

"You can go to hell!"

Potts shoved his body around to face Linton. "If I ain't found someone I like less by midnight, Linton, I'm gonna have the boys pick you up. If only for insultin' an officer of the New York Police Department. We don't need you this morning no more. Exit."

Linton passed a glance at Steve. Steve turned away and sat down. Linton left.

"Tell us any more, Mr. Levy?" Potts asked with a sigh.

"No." Steve was abrupt.

"All right. Do you know Charlie Beach?"

"Yes."

"When did you see him last?"

"A couple of days ago."

Potts reflected on the answer. "Step outside for a minute, Mr. Levy."

Steve walked out slowly.

"Mr. Boley. What about you?"

Bill looked at Frank intently. The man's usually flushed face was white and tight. A heavy whisky smell emerged when he talked.

"I was in the box-office from seven-thirty on."

"Did you see Charlie Beach lately?"

"Last night." Boley looked inquiringly at Bill.

"You can tell him, Frank," Bill said.

"Bill brought him to the box-office last night in the third act. Charlie threatened to make a fuss. He wanted to get even with Leo. Bill stopped him."

Potts glanced at Bill with a new light in his eyes.

"Mr. Boley, you knew that Murray was at Bill's room at the Chicopee, didn't you?"

Boley looked puzzled. "No."

"But you had a note in the box-office from Murray to Mac-Monnies. Leo told where he was in that note. Didn't you read it?"

"No."

"The note was open when you gave it to Bill."

Boley rose angrily. His face was red. He took a step toward Bill. "Benedict, you're trying to wangle me in on this. You know damn' well I wouldn't touch Leo." He was breathing hard.

"I'm not wangling you in on anything," Bill said.

"Keep your shirt tucked in, Boley," Potts warned.

"I didn't know where Leo was, and if I did I wouldn't have done harm to him."

"That's fine, Boley. You hang around the office today. I'll want to talk to you later, maybe."

Boley went out angrily. He slammed the door behind him. Potts opened it and called Steve in.

Steve, biting at a pipe, walked over to a chair and sat down.

Potts filled his mouth with chewing gum. "What time did Linton and Lawrence come to the theater last night?"

"About eight-thirty. I told you before. Bill can verify that."

"That's right, Potts," Bill said. "Steve was worried that Lawrence would be late for her entrance cue."

"Did they come in a cab?"

"Yes," said Bill.

"What kind of a cab?"

Steve was silent.

"What kind of a cab, Bill?"

"To be honest, I didn't notice."

"The same with me, Mr. Potts," Steve added.

"Why lie, kid?"

"Linton said he came in a Terminal," Steve said.

"But it wasn't a Terminal, was it?"

Steve looked down at his pipe.

"Come on, Steve," Bill said. "Tell him what you know, if you know anything."

"I'll lose my job."

"The hell with a job, Levy. We're trying to find a murderer."

"Yeah . . . that's easy. But find a job these days. I got a wife and kid."

"It don't have to go no further than me. Be a good guy and tell me."

"It was a Yellow."

"Thanks, Steve." Potts made a note. "And don't worry, kid."

Steve left them.

Potts rubbed his hands together. "What a bunch of screwballs."

"Have you seen MacMonnies?"

"Saw him this morning. Before coming here. No soap, Bill. From eight to eight-thirty, Mr. MacMonnies was at his apartment. He gave me the names of ten people, some of 'em pretty respectable. They'll vouch for him."

Bill threw his cigarette away in disappointment. "I'm a stinking detective."

Potts smiled. "You'll learn if you're with me long. I may not be any educated, word-spoutin' Philo Vance. I don't take dope like Sherlock Holmes. I don't love orchids like that fat slob, Nero Wolfe. But I'll be a four-star pretzel-bender if I'm as dumb as the cops they got as stooges in them stories."

"What do you do now?"

Potts sat down and looked at his notes. "I don't say no one is outta consideration. Miss Murray, Linton—that boy lied—Boley— he's a hot Irishman with a lot of griddles in his pants." He paused, his jaws slacked off. "Who owns *Hour's End?*"

"Linton's got a big sock of it. Murray owned the rest."

"Who'd get anything by bumpin' off Leo?"

"The only one I can think of is his sister. Unless a wife turns up one of these days."

Potts grunted. The telephone rang. The detective answered it. After a moment, he hung up with a bang.

"Charlie Beach," he said. "Charlie Beach has disappeared."

Bill grunted and pulled a pack of cigarettes out of his pocket.

"He didn't get home to sleep last night. His landlady says he called her this morning to tell her he was leaving town."

"The damned fool!" Bill said.

CHAPTER VII
GREEKS BEAR GIFTS

In an Italian restaurant on 59th Street Bill was laying out some knives and forks on the table in front of him.

"What are you doing with the silverware?" Sue asked.

Bill pointed to a sugar bowl at the center of the table. "Let that represent Leo Murray. The knives represent all the possible suspects."

"Knives, naturally."

"Those with their points toward the sugar bowl stand for the suspects who were free, as far as we know, at the time of the murder. They are, in order of appearance, Ricky Linton, Alice Lawrence, Charlie Beach, Ruth Murray . . . *and* Nick Finley."

"What about MacMonnies?" Sue asked.

"He's this slightly nicked knife with the blunt end facing the sugar. He has an alibi. So have Frank Boley and Steve Levy."

"So have I and so have you. So have the United States Marines."

A tall, stout man with a Dutchman's beer-red face entered the restaurant and walked over to Bill's table.

"Hello, Bill."

"Hello, Happy. Happy Vorhaus, Miss Huxley."

Sue smiled and Happy shook her hand vigorously.

"Well, so long, Happy," Bill said.

"Thanks, Bill," said Happy. "I'd be glad to join you for a bite to eat."

Bill shrugged helplessly. "Leave us alone, Happy. Can't you see I'm trying to make Miss Huxley?"

"If Miss Huxley," said the fat man, "would let herself be made by a rubber-hearted press agent like you, nothing I can do by my presence will affect your tête-a-tête in any way."

"Sit down, Mr. Vorhaus," Sue said. "You've won a blue ribbon for the best description of the year."

Happy Vorhaus was perhaps the best-known ticket speculator in New York. Compared to Vorhaus, Leblang's Cut Rate ticket office was strictly amateur. He had his pudgy thumb in most theatrical pies, and his yearly income tax was limited only by the number of nephews and nieces he supported.

"Who could have murdered Leo?" Happy asked.

"Who'll be the next president, Happy?"

"Ah—Professor Quiz," said Sue.

"What are you going to do now?" Happy asked. "I mean by way of a job."

"I'm going to hang on as long as they pay me."

"I don't think that's going to be long."

"How come?"

"The dope is . . . Ricky Linton's arranging to hire someone else. That gives you the well-known gate." Happy puffed up his cheeks to denote the importance of his words. "He don't like you, Bill."

"I know."

"How could anyone fail to fall or fall to fail for Bill Benedict?" Sue asked with a limb of celery sticking out impertinently from her full lips.

"People have blind-spots," Bill said. "Got another job for me, Happy?"

"Yes."

"Probably want you to publicize the new python they got at the zoo," Sue said.

"Nick Finley asked me to find him an up and coming p.a. for a new show of his going into rehearsal next month."

"What happened to Dick Maney?" asked Bill.

"Going to Hollywood. Sam Goldwyn is running out of mistakes."

Bill sat back in his seat. "Why didn't Nick ask me himself."

"Being that Leo and Nick was not exactly on talking terms, Nick thought that you might hesitate before going over to him. So he asked me to kind of broach it to you."

"Good old Happy," Bill said. "Always ready to jump into the broach."

"Ignore it and have some spaghetti, Mr. Vorhaus," Sue said, passing the platter to the fat man. "Who do you think finished off Leo?"

Happy took a large helping and stuffed his mouth full once or twice before answering. Then he drawled:

"I'd say I was the only man in New York who didn't hate his guts."

"Like Caesar's wife, eh?"

"It's all right with me." Vorhaus finished the spaghetti and lit a cigar. "What about the Finley job, Bill?"

Bill spun the sugar bowl thoughtfully. "I'll ask Ruth Murray if it's okay with her. If it is, I go to work for Nick. Three hundred a week."

"Okay," said Happy quickly and rose. "I'll tell him. I know he'll be glad." He bowed to Sue. "Pleased to have met you."

When Happy was out of the restaurant, Sue clinched her cigarette and said, "Bill, that's two hundred a week more than Leo gave you."

"Yeah, I know, little one. So does Happy. Something's on the air. Finley never paid a p.a. as much as that before. It's not because I'm so good."

"Oh no, it couldn't be that."

Bill tapped her wrist with a knife. "If the Greeks bear gifts, they'd better be good ones."

CHAPTER VIII
A DEAD MURDERER ARISES

The funeral was held that afternoon at the Riverside Memorial Chapel. The pews were garnished with as many celebrities as could get away from other funerals. Among those present "to pay their respects to the theatrical genius of Leo Murray" as the papers somewhat equivocally put it were all the everybodys who get their names in Ed Sullivan's, Leonard Lyons' and Winchell's columns.

Hake Potts was standing around as unobtrusively as the World's Fair. He saw Bill and came over to him.

"Seen Charlie Beach?"

"Not unless he's hiding in Helen Morgan's new hairdress."

Potts tried to whisper, "I'm sending out a statewide alarm."

Someone near by grunted angrily, "*Please!* This is a funeral."

Potts lowered the creases of his face into a saint-like expression and folded his large, red hands in front of him.

The services ended and people began to file into the funeral cars to go out to the cemetery.

Alice Lawrence, dressed in a pair of silver foxes, came over to Bill.

"God, wasn't it wonderful?" she gushed.

Bill started to walk away. She grabbed his arm. "This is the first Leo Murray production I really liked."

Bill drove back from the cemetery with Potts. The detective was glum. He chewed incessantly.

"It relieves the nervous pressure," Potts said, feeling he owed Bill an explanation.

"I gather then, that the Leo Murray mystery is still as much of a mystery as it was."

"Who the hell do you think I am? He was murdered last night at eight. Less than twenty-four hours ago. All I have to do is think and deduct and deduct and think, then make an arrest, eh? Hell, I haven't spoken to the cast. I haven't seen Charlie Beach. And why ain't you been honest with me?"

"Old Honest Bill is what they call me."

"Whyn't you tell me about Nick Finley?"

"Tell what?"

Potts crumpled a piece of cellophane and threw it away angrily. "Don't you ever read Winchell?"

"Not on weekdays."

"It says Finley and Murray had a fight yesterday at Sardi's. You was there."

"So I was. A lot of guys have had fights with Murray before."

"But Murray wasn't murdered before." Potts glanced sideways at Bill. "I saw Finley early this afternoon."

"What's his story?"

"He says he was at the theater from about eight-thirty on. And in Central Park walking alone from eight to eight-thirty. How in the name of honesty can a guy check on a story like that?" Potts massaged his gums and continued casually. "He wanted to know what you were doing at that time."

"Me?"

"He asked it offhand."

Bill smiled pleasantly. "Very interesting. And only at lunch today he had an emissary ask me if I wanted to work for him. . . . I think Mr. Finley needs a little going over. He's on my list."

"The law's done all it can."

"Who said anything about the law?"

Bill promised Potts to be at the theater at eleven that night for the cross-examination of the cast. They left each other at 50th Street and Broadway. Bill got Sue Huxley on the phone.

"Let's eat together tonight," he said.

"Who we going to eat?"

"Cut the airy nothings, my headache, and meet me at Lindy's at six-thirty."

Bill walked over to a Western Union and sent a wire to Nick Finley. Then he returned to the office. The door was locked. He let himself in with his pass key. He picked up a pack of telegrams of condolence which had accumulated since the morning and opened them.

One telegram made him stop and whistle. He put it in his pocket carefully and dialed Potts' precinct house. The detective wasn't in.

"Any message?" the desk sergeant asked.

Bill bit at a nail. "No."

For a few minutes he sat in the darkened office without moving. Then he re-read the telegram and walked to Boley's office. The door was locked. Bill took a paper clip out of his pocket and tried to open the lock with it. The clip bent too easily. He threw it away and walked the rest of the way down the hall to Leo's office. In the door he saw a key. He took it out and tried it on Boley's lock. It worked.

The office was dark. Bill turned up the small desk lamp. He tried all the drawers. They were unlocked. The biggest one had six bottles of Scotch and a hundred or more Lily cups. The other drawers contained old *Varietys* and box-office statements. But in the last one he found something he was looking for: Boley's checkbook.

Bill made a list of people and stores to whom the checks were drawn. One store interested him. The Lionel Company. He was-making a note of the dates of the canceled checks when he heard the outer door opened. Quickly he put the checkbook back in its place, turned out the light, and walked into the hall. It was Ruth.

"Hello. . . ."

Ruth looked up at him, frightened. "Bill! I thought no one was here."

"I came in to knock out a release on . . . on the funeral."

"Oh. . . ."

"Ruth, you oughtn't to hang around here."

Tears filled her eyes. She pulled nervously at her pocketbook. "I can't help it, Bill. This office is so filled with memories of Leo. His voice and his walk and the hundreds of hours we talked about plays, and interviewed actors and playwrights. . . ." She sat down, trembling. "I can't help it. Leo was all I had. . . . I can't stay at home. . . . I'm terribly lonely. . . ."

"Come out to dinner with us. Me and Sue."

She smiled. "Thanks. Not tonight. You and Sue should be alone. . . . Some other night." She looked around the room, her white hands fluttering oddly in the sharp light of the lamp. "There are scripts I ought to send back. I'll keep busy."

"Lots of telegrams came in." Bill offered her a cigarette. She took one and he lit it for her. "All the big shots."

"No personal ones?"

"Leo had mighty few—" He hesitated.

"I have friends."

"Friends don't send telegrams."

She stared at the pile of yellow and blue envelopes. "You're right."

Bill wanted to ask a question. Instead, he said, "Last chance gulch. Come out to eat with us."

She shook her head.

"Good night, Ruth."

"Good night, Bill."

When he got downstairs Bill telephoned Nick Finley.

At Lindy's, Bill and Sue took a table for two. Sue's eyes showed her curiosity. "You look mysterious, Mr. B. I can tell by the way you haven't ordered drinks yet."

He was silent. A waiter came over.

"Four straight Scotches."

"Even more mysterious."

Bill concentrated on the menu. There was a long silence.

Sue said sharply:

"Would you prefer to discuss mid-season fashions? Or do you think ice-hockey will ever take the place of love?"

Bill looked at her abstractedly.

"If it weren't for the fact I was hungry," Sue continued, "I wouldn't dream of asking you about new slants on the Murray case."

"I think you look squiffy tonight, Sue. Your new hair-do looks like you just come fresh out of a shower . . . or out of bed."

"I've come fresh out of a beauty parlor is what you mean, and it's not flattery I'm after."

"You're beautiful."

"No," Sue said.

"No, what?"

"No, I won't marry you."

"Who asked you to?" Bill tried to look upset.

"Then why did you say I looked beautiful?"

Bill slid a napkin off the table onto his lap. "Because someone's got to pay for my dinner. I'm broke."

The waiter brought the four Scotches. Bill drank two quickly. Then: "What'll it be, Sue, Marinierte herring or gefuelte fish for your appetizer?"

"Chopped liver with a delicate sprinkling of onions."

"Two orders of chopped liver," Bill told the waiter. "And a side dish of Listerine." He tried to knock knees with Sue under the table.

"Last time I got housemaid's knee!"

Bill said suddenly. "Can you keep a secret?"

Sue nodded.

'Something entirely off the record, something between you and me . . . or is it you and I?"

"You and me. . . ."

"I read a telegram today from the murderer."

"His name?"

"John Wilkes Booth."

"Oh they finally got him, did they? Mrs. Lincoln will be glad to hear it."

"Stupid! I don't mean *the* John Wilkes Booth."

"Oh, little junior. I always say, like father like son."

"Just hold everything . . . and listen." He drank the third Scotch, took the telegram out of his pocket and handed it to her.

RUTH MURRAY   1131A 156P R108
REGENT THEATER BUILDING
NEW YORK
WHAT YOUR BROTHER RECEIVED YOU ALSO
CAN RECEIVE. SUGGEST YOU CLOSE HOUR'S
END IMMEDIATELY. BEST RETURNS OF THE
DAY.
                                   JOHN WILKES BOOTH.

"It might be a crank," Sue said thoughtfully.

"It might be from the murderer. It's a little too early for Mother's Day."

"Who gets anything by closing *Hour's End?*"

"The actors wouldn't. Linton wouldn't. He owns half the show. Certainly not MacMonnies."

"Nick Finley?"

"The more hits, the better it is for every producer in town. He's not nuts."

"Has Ruth seen it?"

"No. What's the point in worrying her? I called Potts but he wasn't in. I'll give it to him tonight. Maybe he'll put a man to guard her."

Sue swallowed some water. "It may be the telegram, or it may only be the onions, but I feel hot all over. There's certainly a murderer at large."

Bill split a piece of toast in his hands. "Maybe Potts can trace the wire."

"I have an idea, Bill!" She dropped a spoon to the floor in her excitement. "A really good idea!"

"I know. You think the wire was sent by Charlie Beach."

Sue looked down at her food in disgust.

Bill grinned. "Hell, even Father Brown would have gotten that right off. But here's something that's harder. What's The Lionel Company best known for?"

"Toys. Electric trains."

Bill nodded. "Now, examine what you know about Leo Murray. His character and personality."

"He's definitely not the kind of a man who builds a railroad system in his back yard."

"How about buying gifts for his friends' kids?"

"He didn't believe in children. . . . Pass the cream, Bill."

"In Frank Boley's checkbook . . . in the account he ran for Leo Murray, I found the stubs of several checks drawn to the order of The Lionel Company."

Sue made a sound with her lips. "I begin to smell . . ."

"Those were the onions, dear. . . ."

"Pass the cream!"

"My instinct," said Bill, "leads me to look up all the Murrays in the marriage records at City Hall first thing in the morning. Want to meet me there?"

"When?"

"Eleven." Bill was reaching for his hat.

"Where are you going?"

"I've got a date."

"Oh . . . Pardon the intrusion. Two's a crowd."

"I've got to see a man who's a dog."

"Pass the cream!"

"But if you'd like to meet me at the Arcadia at eleven you can watch the cast getting exxed, as Mr. Potts says. He won't like it, but I guess you can hide yourself in a hole."

"A rabbit, eh?"

He leaned over and kissed her. "Here's the cream, rabbit. And don't forget to pay the bill."

CHAPTER IX
FATAL INTERVIEW

Bill found Nick Finley at home waiting for him. Finley lived alone in a penthouse apartment on Central Park South. He met him at the door.

"I got your wire, Bill," he said.

"I thought you'd be here."

"Have a drink?" The stocky man walked over to a cellarette.

"Scotch straight," Bill said. He looked at the room. It was large and furnished in modern style; the chairs and sofa low, the lamps chromium plated, the ash trays, aluminum shovels. Through large glass doors at the end of the room, Bill saw the distant lights of Harlem beyond the dark square of Central Park. A concrete porch about ten feet wide ran the length of the room.

"Nice view, eh?" Finley asked. He handed Bill a drink.

"Beautiful."

"Just think of what would happen if enemy bombers came over."

"Yeah. . . . Good-by, New York."

"Think there'll be a war, Bill?"

Bill looked at Finley. The Irishman's gold rimmed glasses caught the reflection of a near-by lamp. "Hitler's a big-time maniac."

"Sure," Finley agreed. "But I see it something like this." The squat man walked over and sat down on an orange couch that looked like a sunburned salamander. Bill remained standing.

"I see a gang of bankers sitting."

"Where?"

"What the hell diff does it make, where? Sitting, that's all. So they say let's have a war scare. So they have a war scare. Stocks go down and they buy. Let's have a peace wave, they say. So they have a peace wave. Stocks go up and they sell. It's a nice lunch we had. Good day, gentlemen, and they go home. . . ." Bill laughed sourly. "Good joke, eh?"

"I know a better one."

"What's that?"

"You willing to pay me three hundred ice cold buckeroos each week."

Finley moved uneasily on the couch. "Sure. You're worth it."

"For what?"

"For doing your regular p.a. job."

Bill swallowed the rest of the Scotch. "You're a liar, Nick."

Nick got pale. He took off his glasses slowly and wiped them with his handkerchief. "What made you say that?"

Bill grinned. "I think you want to hire me so you can keep your eyes on Bill Benedict. That's what I think."

"You ain't so pretty. I didn't hire you for your beauty."

"What show you plan to do?"

Finley sat back and sighed. "Have another Scotch, Bill."

"Thanks." Bill filled his own glass. "What show, Nick?"

Nick got off the couch and stub-toed across to the bookcase. He tossed a manuscript to Bill. It dropped to the floor. As Bill went to pick it up, Nick slid something from the bookcase into his pocket. It was a service revolver.

Bill wiped his lips with the back of his hand. He threw the manuscript on the couch and lit a cigarette. "*Hour's End*, eh?"

"Yeah."

"What makes you think you can do it?"

"Because it's going to close tomorrow night. The cast has to be changed a bit and I'm going to reopen it."

Bill took the telegram out of his pocket and showed it to Finley. "Is that why you sent this? To frighten Ruth Murray so she'll sell out her share quick?"

Finley read it and began to tremble. He took his glasses off and wiped them. "I didn't send it. For Christ's sake, Bill. I didn't have to send it . . . I already own Linton's share."

"You're a liar!"

"I bought him out this morning." Bill bit his nail. "I wouldn't send such a telegram. You think I'm crazy?"

"What about Leo Murray's share?"

"I don't need Leo's share. Linton had sixty per cent. That's enough." Finley went over to his desk. "I'll show you our deal." He brought out a piece of lawyer's paper. "Look."

Bill glanced through the sheet. "Why would Linton sell?"

"Because the guy's lousy with money. He wants to marry Alice Lawrence and go to Italy with her for a honeymoon. He don't need the chicken feed the play'll give him."

"Fine chicken feed," Bill said. "It'll make a half a million, if it makes a cent."

"Maybe not with Alice Lawrence out of it."

"You still got Nina Gale."

"She's all right but she can't pull 'em in by herself. I'm going to try to get Ina Claire for Lawrence's part."

"You going to keep the revised third act in?"

Finley stared at him. He sat down suddenly.

"Well, are you going to keep the revised act or not?" He looked sharply at Finley. Finley smiled weakly.

"What revised third act?" he asked.

Bill grinned. He put his glass back on the table and walked over to Nick.

"Don't you know about the revisions in Act Three, Scene Three?"

Nick waved him away. "Sure. . . . MacMonnies told me."

"He did, heh? What are they?"

"Oh . . . Hell! I don't want to discuss 'em. I don't like 'em." Finley started to rise.

"Oh, you don't like 'em," Bill said pushing him back. "You don't like them because you never saw them. And you never saw them because they were done for the first time last night right before the final curtain."

"Sure," said Nick.

"Sure. Now that I've told you, you remember. But you didn't remember a minute ago because you left the theater before the final curtain to sneak up to my room in the Chicopee to kill Leo Murray."

"You're crazy!" Nick screamed.

Bill reached over and tore Nick's glasses off his face. With his other hand he smacked it hard . . . and again. "Don't you remember, Nick? I came in and you got scared . . . and you smacked me." He jerked Finley off the couch and rapped knuckles across his chin. The short man fell to the floor. "Do you remember how you knocked me out?" Finley dove his hand into his pocket for the revolver. Bill saw it in time and jumped him. He pinned Nick's hand to the floor and socked a knee into his crotch. Nick squealed. The revolver fell from his trembling fingers.

"Stop it!" he yelled. "You'll kill me!"

"You killed Leo Murray and tried to finish me off!" Bill slid his fingers around Nick's fat throat. "You did, didn't you?"

Nick gasped. "I'll tell . . . you . . . . Let . . . me. . . up."

Bill released his hold and pulled Finley to his feet. He picked up the gun and put it in his pocket. "Sure, you'll tell me."

Nick sunk his body on the couch. "Get me a drink," he said weakly.

"You don't have any more of these toys around, do you?" He pointed to the gun in his pocket. Finley shook his head. Then Bill walked over and poured out a glass of Scotch for Finley, and one for himself. Bill drank silently. Finley was still trying to catch his breath.

"Where are my glasses?" His blue, nearsighted eyes blinked. Bill got them for him. Heavy drops of perspiration dripped from Finley's bald dome. Bill pulled the producer's handkerchief out of his breast-pocket. "Here," he said, "wipe yourself, you're wet all over."

"What about . . . the revisions? Did you trip me up . . . or are they a fact?"

"The real McCoy. Alice played her lines as she wanted . . . and Steve Levy, the stage manager, crossed Leo and didn't pull down the curtain. If you were there you'd know the lines had been changed. You know that play as well as Leo did. He stole it from you, didn't he?"

"Sure, he stole it."

"And you killed him."

"I didn't kill him. I swear I didn't."

"But you were in my room."

Finley drank some of the whisky and coughed. "Yes, I went to kill him, but . . . I found Leo dead when I arrived."

"You sure must have been careful that no one saw you," Bill said.

"I walked up from the men's room in the basement."

"How did you know he was in my room?"

"I saw him on his way over. We had a drink at Nedick's at the corner." Finley wiped his head. "I begged him for ten per cent. A million dollars he stole from me. Like *Grand Hotel* or *Our Town*. The least he could do was to cut me in. I was willing to pay for it but Leo was a guy without a heart. Something you step on before it bites you. A cockroach, a scab, a louse."

"Cut out the eulogy. What did you do then?"

"I had a bite to eat and went to the show. That's a kind of nut I am. I like to pinch myself to feel it hurt. My million dollars going into another man's pocket. You kill for less than that. I sat through the first two acts of the play like a man sitting on fire. I met you in the intermission, remember?"

"Yes."

"I didn't go back into the theater but walked around like a crazy man, maybe for an hour. Then I went over to the Chicopee. I planned to see Leo secretly without no one seeing me. I was going to threaten to kill him unless he gave me a share of the show." Finley was trembling. "Maybe I would've killed him. I don't know. My God, I don't know. I got into the room. The lights were on. I saw him on the floor, the knife sticking into his back like a tooth-pick in an olive. Then I heard the elevator and steps coming to the door. I turned out the light quickly and picked up a book-end."

Bill touched his temple.

"I had sense enough to wipe my fingerprints off the book-end, and then I beat it down the stairs."

"And waited for the morning papers, eh?"

"I didn't kill Leo!"

"Will the cops believe you?"

"Bill, for Chrissake, you ain't going to tell 'em, are you?"

"Sure." Bill got his hat and put it on.

"Bill. . . . It'll kill me. . . . It'll kill my reputation. . . . I won't be able to stand it." Bill walked to the door relentlessly. "I'll give you a cut of the show, if you shut up."

"How big a cut?"

Finley's eyes narrowed for a moment, then: "Two per cent."

"You cheap skate. For two per cent, you want me to save you from the chair?"

"Five per cent," Finley bid, breathing hard.

"Not for your whole sixty per cent," Bill replied. "I wanted to see how cheap you really are. But I'll take your offer of the job beginning tomorrow. I can use the dough to open my agency again."

"But you won't tell the cops?" Finley kept wiping his chin with a fine linen handkerchief.

"Where were you at eight o'clock last night?"

Finley's lips twisted craftily. "Walking in Central Park. I told that to Potts."

"Yeah, that's what you told him. What do you tell me?"

"The same thing, Bill. I swear to God. Central Park."

"Alone?"

Finley hesitated. "Yes."

"Okay. I won't tell Potts—yet." Bill opened the door and took the revolver out of his pocket. He looked at it and pointed it at Finley. The producer cringed. "If you try anything funny, my friend, I'm going to give you over to Potts—in pieces. Good night."

Bill threw the revolver on the salamander couch and left. He hopped an Eighth Avenue bus for the theater.

CHAPTER X
"ALL COPS AIN'T PHILO VANCES"

Potts was out in front of the stage entrance with some plainclothes men when Bill arrived at the Arcadia.

"Picked up Charlie Beach yet?" Bill asked.

"Nope," Potts replied sullenly. "He's probably living next door to the 52nd Street police station. It's the safest place for a wantee. We cops ain't learnt yet to scratch in our back yards."

"An admission, Lieutenant. I thought—"

"Ice it and put it away, what you thought. All cops ain't dumb, and all cops ain't Philo Vances. Where would you go if you were hiding out?"

"Who, me?"

"Listen, when I become a ventriloquist I'll tell you."

"My, you're in a bad mood, Lieutenant."

"I'm working myself up for the exxing I got to give when the curtain falls."

"Stanislaysky used a method like that."

Potts looked at Bill sharply. "What detective story writer manufactured him? I gotta keep up with literature."

"He's a Russian—"

"Oh, a Red, huh."

"A Russian stage director who is now dead."

Potts removed some gum from his shoes. "Some people are careless where they throw it." He turned to Bill. "Where would you go if you were trying to hide from the cops?"

Bill thought a minute. "If I had the money, I'd take a suite in the New York Athletic Club."

"Good," said Potts grudgingly.

"But if I were penniless, I'd make it my business to get run in for vagrancy and stay safely hidden in the Tombs or some place."

"That's even better."

"But," Bill smiled, "if I were Charlie Beach with a little money in my pockets, I'd spend my days in the Drama Exhibit Rooms at Columbia University Library, and my nights in a fifteen-cent movie house on 42nd Street."

"I'll go up to Columbia tomorrow, myself," Potts muttered.

"You flatter me, Lieutenant."

The big man's face opened in a grin. "It's because I got you trained."

"No doubt."

People were beginning to seep through the Arcadia's doors.

Jimmy Burke came over to the detective. "It's curtain time, Mr. Potts."

"Don't let no newspaper boys in, Burke," Potts ordered and went back-stage followed by his plainclothes men.

Bill remained outside and looked for Sue Huxley. She wasn't around. He recognized a flock of second string critics, the wire-service boys, the left-boys, the weekly and the monthly boys. Joe Krutch of *The Nation* looking like an El Greco in modern dress was talking to Kyle Crichton of *Colliers*.

Through the crowd, Bill saw Broadway Rose shuffling along. Her eyes, as usual, were hungrily searching the sidewalk. For what? No one ever knew. Rose was a Broadway fixture. She walked the street twenty-four hours a day in the same gray, dirty coat and the same straggling, ratty hair slipping down over her face. Few people saw her face because she kept it averted and looking down. In her thin hands she held an inevitable package of chewing gum. No one ever bought any from her, but no one of the Broadway citizens ever passed her by without giving her a nickel.

She slithered up to Bill.

"Hello, Rose." He gave her a coin.

She grunted.

"How are you feeling?"

"Good." Her voice was like her hair, ratty.

"Rose, why don't you ever look up in the sky?"

"I never lost nothin' there."

Bill smiled and turned away. She caught his arm. "Mister."

"Yeah . . ."

She pointed to a taxi with her box. "There's a guy in there. He wants to see you."

Bill looked at the cab quickly. He couldn't see anyone in the back but he recognized the driver.

"Thanks." He patted Rose's arm and walked over. Bill looked in. Laney was there. "Hop in, Benedict," he said. Bill shrugged and entered.

"Drive around the block, buddy," Laney instructed the driver.

"What is this, Laney? A snatch?"

"A joy ride, Benedict. Around the block. I wanna talk to you." He took some match-boxes out of his pocket and shuffled them in his hands.

"A hobby, Laney?" Bill asked.

Laney smiled sheepishly. His teeth gleamed white and even. "Yeah . . . Got thousands of 'em."

Bill smiled. "Never suspect it. Shows that every man has his weakness. Achilles' heel."

"What d'ya mean heel?" Laney's face darkened. Bill put up a protesting hand. "I don't mean you. Just an old Greek friend."

The gangster thought it over a minute, then grinned. "No hard feelings, Benedict?"

"None."

The taxi was squirming its way past a red light on Eighth Avenue. Bill glanced at his watch. It was getting late. Potts would be through before he got back. "What's on your mind, Laney?" Bill inquired gently.

"Was you a friend of Murray's? The guy that got stuck?"

"Yes."

"How much buys the name of the guy who hired me to t'row stink bombs the night his show opened?"

Bill laughed. "You didn't."

"I was gonna. Ya stopped me. Remember?"

"I remember."

"How much?"

"I got some of those match covers at home. I'll give ten."

Laney twisted in his seat. "That ain't funny."

Bill nodded. "I know a joke when I see one. What did you actually want to speak to me about?"

Laney opened his lips angrily to say something. He changed his mind.

"What, Laney?" Bill lit a cigarette and leaned back on the seat.

"You're a smart guy, Benny. They ought to put you in the movies."

Bill leaned forward and knocked at the window separating the driver from him. "Take me back to the Arcadia, buddy," he said.

"Wait a minute," Laney said quickly.

"I'll give you once more around the block, Laney," Bill warned.

Laney hesitated and bit at his thumb nail. "Will ya gimme five grand if I put my finger on the nose of the guy who knifed Murray?"

Bill puffed his cigarette smugly. "Make it two."

"Five or go to hell."

"Three."

"Five!"

"Thirty-five hundred."

Laney yelled to the cab-driver. "Pull up at the corner!" When the taxi stopped, Bill got out on the sidewalk but kept the door open.

"What do you say, Laney?" he asked. "Thirty-five hundred?"

"I told ya five! I need five! Ya don't gimme it, I get it somewhere else!"

Bill sighed. "Okay. When?"

Laney concentrated on a blue-green match cover advertising a new gin. "Gimme a couple of days."

"Take all the time you want, Laney," Bill said and left.

Potts had ordered the curtain lowered. The cast and stage crew were scattered around the various prop chairs and couches. In one corner sat Alice Lawrence looking amused and slightly drunk, her brunette hair glossy from the amber and rose spotlights that were on her. Standing near her was Ricky Linton in evening clothes. They were talking together in whispers, and now and then Alice put her white hand on his arm and rubbed it in an exciting way. Seated with his dresser, Farley, was Sir Basil Gilbert. He was still in his make-up. Nina Gale was leaning forward, intently studying Potts' gestures.

Potts stood center stage checking over a list of the company and stage-hands with Steve Levy. When he finished he ordered one of the plainclothes men to make sure no one was around who didn't belong. Then he faced the cast.

"Ladies and gentlemen, I'm Lieutenant Potts. I got questions to ask you. It would take all night to put 'em and get 'em from each one of you separately. So I'm going to ask the whole gang at the same time. It's unusual but it'll have to do. And take it for granted, I want the truth." The detective wiped his mouth with the palm of his hand. Bill, who stood a little in back of him, could see that Potts surreptitiously spat his chewing gum into his hand, transferring it a moment later to a piece of cellophane and putting it in his vest pocket.

"The first question is this." Potts glanced at a slip of paper. "Who was out of this theater last night between seven-thirty and eight o'clock eliminating Miss Lawrence and Mr. Linton?"

There was a long silence. Hara stepped forward. "I was. I went out for some coffee. Just for a minute." He turned to his buddy. "Ain't that so, Andy?"

"That's right, chief."

"Okay," said Potts. "I believe you. Anybody else."

Again, a long pause. The detective kept his eyes on his paper. "All right," he said, finally. "Anybody here have personal dealings with Leo Murray apart from getting work from him or knowing him just around the theater? Anybody know anything about his personal life? . . . Just say yes. Don't go into details."

No one answered.

"No one knows nothing, eh?"

Again there was silence.

Potts chuckled and threw some pieces of gum in his mouth. "Okay. You asked for it. Rabinowitz! Take Miss Lawrence to her dressing room. See that she don't leave. McNally!" He called another detective. "Do the same for Mr. Linton here. Both of 'em are liars."

Ricky Linton strode angrily toward Potts. Before he had a chance to smack a fist into the detective's face, McNally grabbed him.

"Throw him in a dressing room," Potts ordered. "If he don't like it, dirty that starched shirt of his."

Linton stepped up to Potts defiantly. "And you'll be walking a beat in Queens."

Potts laughed. "Everybody from Dutch Schultz, up and down, has threatened me with Queens and I'm still on Broadway. And, anyway, what the hell's wrong with Queens? I live there."

A couple of the stage-hands laughed.

"I want to see a lawyer," Alice Lawrence cried shrilly.

"I'm not arresting you, Miss. Holding you just temporarily for questioning. Maybe, when I'm through you can get a lawyer."

The detectives took them away.

Potts walked the length of the stage and leaned against the proscenium. "The rest of you can go. . . ."

Potts brought Linton and Lawrence together in one dressing room. Bill stood at the door watching their expressions as reflected in the make-up mirrors which covered one wall, watching Linton who kept scratching at his cigarette lighter, turning it on and blowing it out, and Alice wetting her lips constantly.

The detective sat down, stretched his thick legs and pointed a stick of gum at Linton. "Why'd ya hit Murray yesterday?"

Ricky suddenly relaxed. "He insulted Miss Lawrence."

"That's a fair reason. That wouldn't be enough to murder Murray?"

Alice laughed hysterically.

"What's so funny?"

"If all the actresses insulted by Leo Murray were put together in one room—"

"You'd have a Goldwyn Follies' chorus," Bill completed.

"Linton, why did ya lie to me about coming in a Terminal cab?" Potts asked.

"I didn't lie."

"It was a Yellow."

"I'm not in the habit of making entries in my diary as to what kind of cab I take."

"You knew it was a Yellow but ya didn't want me to check where ya took it from. You're a fool, Linton. When Terminal had no record of a trip from Sheridan Square to the Arcadia Theater, I tried the other companies. Hell, even the driver recognized you, Miss Lawrence." Potts opened his notebook. "Ya got on at 65th Street and Fifth Avenue at ten minutes past eight. What were ya doing at 65th Street?"

"My lawyer'll tell you," Linton said.

"You'll tell me." Potts stuck out his elephantine jaw stubbornly.

Alice leaned over to Linton. "Don't let this Tammany ward-heel make you say anything you don't want to."

Potts reddened. "Save your wisecracks for an audience. . . . What were ya doing on the street where Leo Murray lived?"

Linton screwed in a gadget on his lighter. Alice wet her lips and scrawled aimlessly on the dressing table with a make-up pencil.

"What was Leo Murray to ya, Miss Lawrence?"

She lifted her large eyes to the detective. "I've forgotten."

Potts stood up angrily. "Ya begged for it. Now, try to forget this. Leo Murray's been giving ya a weekly check for the last three years. Maybe he was just a good Samaritan—sit down, Linton!"

"Like hell I will." He lifted a cologne bottle and threw it at the detective. Potts ducked, kicked over a chair that stood in front of him and slammed a round, brick-like fist into Linton's jaw. Linton staggered. Alice screamed and swung her handbag at Potts. With one hand the detective caught hold of Linton's arm and twisted it. With the other, he rapped at the man's mouth until blood oozed between his lips.

"Let him go! You're killing him!" Alice shrieked.

"Call a cop, why don't ya," Potts grunted. Linton slumped on the floor, semiconscious.

"He got only what I promised him. And, lady, ya can call a cop if ya want, but I warn ya: there's only one place in this country where a cop won't protect ya . . . and that's in a police station."

"What do you want from us?" said Alice. She was kneeling at Linton's side, wiping the blood from his lips. Potts and Bill picked the man up and sat him on a chair.

"I want the truth. Why did ya break into Murray's apartment house the night of the murder?"

"Why do you ask such questions?"

"My system, I keep to myself. What did ya want from Murray?"

She looked at Linton. He lowered his eyelids and made a slight move with his head.

"We did not break into Mr. Murray's apartment. We weren't anywhere near it."

Linton got to his feet. "And put that on your Victrola and play it."

"What was ya looking for?"

"She told you we weren't there," Linton said.

"Ya were."

"Prove it. Get the D.A. to draw up a complaint of breaking and entering. Let's see your evidence."

Potts kept his sad eyes on Linton's face.

"Well . . . what's your evidence?"

The detective chewed silently.

"If you got some, why don't you arrest us?" Alice said, walking to the door insolently.

"I make my own plans, Miss Lawrence," the detective said.

Linton opened the door. "Come on, Alice. Let's get out of here. Unless . . ." He turned to Potts. "Unless the cops would like to stop us."

"No," said Potts. "I give ya the freedom of the city. As for the squabble, fair exchange's not even petty larceny."

They went out. Potts sat down heavily and rubbed his fist.

"Well . . ." Bill said.

"Well . . . ?" Potts asked.

"Well!" Sue said, standing at the door. "I thought you were having a date with me, Bill."

"Let's all three have a date," Potts said.

CHAPTER XI
MR. POTTS GOES TO TOWN

Potts took Bill and Sue to a room he had in the New Yorker Hotel. It served him as a place to sleep when he worked late. He poured out some Irish pot-still whisky, took off his coat and put on a flowery smoking jacket.

"A long night of talk?" Sue asked, gulping her drink down fast.

"What did ya want with me today when ya called, Bill?" Potts asked.

"I've got a hook for us. To hang something on."

"I thought they electrocuted murderers in this state," Sue said, pouring another drink for herself.

Potts glared at her. "Miss Huxley, you're here because you're a friend of Bill's. If ya know shorthand take down what I say. If not, ya keep those lips of yours—"

"Pretty lips."

"Pretty lips, then. Keep them zippered tight." He tossed over a package of gum. "This'll keep ya busy."

"I'll take shorthand instead. Besides, this is interesting liquor, Mr. Potts. Very interesting. It would spoil chewing gum."

Potts gave her a pencil and pad. "Now take this down. I went over this morning to Leo Murray's apartment. His sister called me to say she thought someone broke into her apartment during the night. She wasn't sure of the time but when she got home from the show, she noticed something was wrong. I took a quick look around. Nothing was missing. But someone had been fooling with Leo's desk. I couldn't figure out what for until I found these in a wastepaper basket." He tossed a package of canceled checks to

Bill. "They're made out to Alice Lawrence and dated the fifteenth of each month. I put two and two together—"

"You mean you put Alice and Leo together," Sue said, taking an absent-minded sip of the Irish.

"And decided that he had been keeping her. It was easy to check on their cab story. They took a Yellow from East 65th Street to the Arcadia. Now, I says, what was they doing in Murray's baili-wick? The canceled checks, I says. So tonight I tried to bluff them into giving themselves away. It didn't work but I know I was right. If I could find a motive for it, I'd be surer."

"It's simple," Bill said. "Ricky and Alice are going to get married. Alice wanted to get those canceled checks back so Leo couldn't use them to blackmail her or Ricky."

"That fits nicely," said Potts. "Get that down, Miss Huxley, will ya?"

"Sure . . . sure." She passed her empty glass to Bill. "Fill this . . . for me, darling."

"You're taking too much, Sue."

"Fill it, darling."

He poured a couple of baby fingers.

"That Leo man is sure some man," Sue whispered blissfully.

"You don't admire him, do you?" Bill demanded.

"I can admire a . . . a man-eating tiger without wantin' to live with him, can't I?"

"Is Linton on the roll of honor?" Bill asked.

The detective nodded. "He ain't scratched yet. Suppose we keep adding A to B. Suppose we say that not finding the canceled checks and knowing that Leo is at your place, they go over. He threatens blackmail. Linton loses his temper which he does fre-quent and picking up your handy Boy Scout knife sticks it into Murray's backside."

Sue applauded.

"I'm just deducting, that's all. Like them crossword puzzles. You don't know a word but you stick something in to see if it fits. If it does, okay. If it don't you try something else." Potts unbut-toned his shoes and hoisted his feet up to a bureau top. "Here's something else. The Medical Examiner can tell approximately the height and strength of a murderer by studying the angle of the wound. For example—" Potts got up and turned Bill around, back facing him. He took a pencil out of his pocket. "The natural hitting stroke with a knife is down, from above your shoulder . . . down."

The detective raised the pencil above his head and stabbed Bill in the back.

"Hey! I haven't got accident insurance!"

"We figured from the way Murray was lying he had his back turned, and the murderer jabbed the knife a little way under Leo's cervical vertebra a bit to the left. If the killer was shorter, the knife would have gone in lower. Here—" Potts put the pencil in Sue's hand. "Now, Miss Huxley, you stab Benedict."

"With pleasure," Sue said. She tiptoed carefully toward Bill.

"You can't knife me, Sue. We're not married yet."

"Eventually. Why not now?"

"You mean—marry me?" Bill asked incredulous.

"No, knife you." She jabbed the pencil at his back.

It landed about halfway down his spine and snapped.

"That hurt!" Bill shouted.

"You see what I mean?" Potts said triumphantly. "She hit you every bit of five inches lower than I did. That's because she's shorter."

"God help me if she were a pigmy."

Sue threw one of Mr. Potts' hotel pillows at him. Bill ducked, and the pillow knocked Mr. Potts' glass of whisky over the bed.

"I'll have you both exiled to Mayor Hague's Siberia. This ain't no play-street."

"Mr. Potts," said Sue pretentiously. "I . . . am profoundly . . . 'pologetic . . . I 'pologize, and beg—"

"Potts, did you find any clues in my room?"

"Some dice and a couple of French postcards."

"A canard. They were given to me." Bill glanced hurriedly at Sue. But she wasn't listening. Her brown eyes with a slight glaze on them were staring hard at the ceiling. Then she tried to rise and put out a wavering hand for help.

"I . . . guess . . . I'm going to . . . pass . . . out . . ." She fell gently to the floor.

"She sure guessed right," Potts said dryly, as he helped Bill carry her to the couch. "Never let her even smell Irish whisky again. It's death to female reporters."

While Sue was moored to the couch by a tidal-wave of sleep that made a mere unconsciousness seem like an American Legion convention, Bill took the John Wilkes Booth telegram out of his pocket and gave it to Potts, who read it and worked the gum in his mouth reflectively.

"Can you find out who sent it?" Bill asked.

"No murderer leaves his name and address and telephone number. The bloke may have phoned it in from a pay station."

"That's fine."

"I'll stick someone on Ruth Murray's tail." Potts waved the telegram. "Sounds like a nut, don't it?"

"Could be Charlie Beach."

"Yeah . . . could be Ricky Linton. Could be Nick Finley."

"No."

Potts opened his eyes wide. "Why not?"

"Nick hasn't the guts."

"It don't take guts to send a wire."

"I mean . . . to kill Leo."

Potts sighed like the exhaust of a Mack truck, then made a squishy sound with his lips. "Between Beach and Linton, I choose Beach."

"On what?"

"Like an artist gets a feeling, that's the way I am. It's a cross between a hunch and a bellyache. Like knowing it'll rain tomorrow. That's the thing I got about this Beach greaseball."

"Charlie was a short guy and as much muscle as a squid. You were counting on a big man."

"Theories got to have holes. The victim might've been bending. The assailant might've jumped. But you can't be too sure. To us, it looks as though Murray was standing with his back toward the killer."

"You mean he trusted the murderer?"

Potts looked at Bill with disgust. "For Chrissake, don't give me none of this mystery story sewerage. The dick says, picking at his nose, 'Who could it be that the victim trusted?' Hell, all his relatives and his friends and his enemies. Take Nick Finley, for example. He probably would've liked to sink his teeth in a piece of Murray. But would Murray be so suspicious he wouldn't turn around for a minute, maybe to reach for a cigarette? Bushwah!"

"You got something there, Mr. Potts."

"You don't get a lieutenant's badge by following baseball scores." Potts yawned and jerked a thumb toward the sleeping Sue. "How about taking your friend home?"

Bill took off one of Sue's shoes and paddled her with it. She sat up suddenly, grabbed her head and moaned, "God, what happened to me?"

Bill winked at Potts who winked back and said, "Congratulations, Mrs. Benedict."

"I couldn't have been that drunk."

"You got yourself into it, young lady." Potts said.

Sue rubbed her aching head and groaned. "I'm just a covered wagon girl, after all."

"I'll see ya to the elevator," Potts said. "I got to make sure the elevator boy don't call a cop to run ya in for disturbing the peace."

When Bill and Sue returned to the Hotel Chicopee, Bill found a note in his mail box.

Bill—

Very important that I see you. I have something to tell you. Make it at the 45th Street end of Shubert's Alley tomorrow night at eleven. Please don't tell cops or anyone and come alone. Please.

Charlie B.

CHAPTER XII
ENTRANCE AND EXIT

When Bill entered the office the next morning he saw that the end of Leo Murray Productions was on the cards. There were no actors and actresses in the outer office. The pile of play scripts which usually hovered over the office like a swaying tower of Babel had been broken up into small piles for return to the various agencies. Ruth, dressed in black, was directing a couple of boys who were packing papers in cardboard cases.

"Is it all over?" Bill said half aloud. Ruth looked into his eyes for a moment without answering. Her face was pale and tight.

"Yes, Bill. Linton's sold out his share of *Hour's End* and there's nothing for me now, except to move Lea's stuff home." She swallowed the hard lump in her throat and turned away.

"If I can help, Ruth—"

Ruth took Bill's hand. "I'm worried, Bill. The man who murdered Leo is still free. And as long as he *is* free, I am not entirely out of danger."

"What makes you think that?"

Ruth dropped her eyes, her hands moving nervously. "I don't know—I just feel it, that's all. . . . I heard about last night at the theater. The police cross-examining the actors. Do you think there's anything in the Linton-Lawrence business? You know, it *is* true that Leo—" She bit her lip and her voice became husky. "Leo—did—was involved with Alice."

"Frankly, I don't know. Potts didn't arrest anybody, and I don't know whether he can or whether he intends to. Not enough evidence."

Ruth sat down at her desk and opened a drawer. She took out a French Line envelop "Here—" She gave it to Bill. It was a ticket for the *Ile de France* made out in the name of Leonard Schary.

"Who is Leonard Schary?"

"A name Leo used. He was going to London."

"But this ticket calls for a sailing the day before yesterday. At midnight. The day he was—killed."

"Yes." Ruth made a slight gesture of her hands. "Leo planned to go abroad. He was keeping it a secret. He intended to retire from the theater and make his home in London."

"Why London?"

"Leo had made enough money to last him the rest of his life. And there were no more worlds to conquer here. He looked forward to buying himself a place in England—and entering society." She laughed sadly. "He even dreamed of entering the Parliament."

"But why did he keep this such a secret?"

"That was Leo's way. It was the most dramatic exit he could think of. Just to disappear and turn up in the House of Lords." She laughed again.

Bill lit a cigarette and made a note on the back of an envelope. The telephone rang. Ruth answered at the switchboard.

"It's for you, Bill," she said, handing him the receiver.

"Hello—"

It was Hake Potts.

"Yeah . . ."

"I just come from that Columbia library. They don't know no Beach."

"Pretty bad guessing."

"Where the hell is he now?" Bill could hear Potts chewing gum viciously.

"What do you mean? How many bad guesses do you give me? Have you tried all those fifteen-cent movie houses on 42nd Street, Mr. Potts?"

"Thanks," said Potts sourly. "You're a help like a hole in my head."

"Be a nice guy, and I may have some important dope on Charlie Beach for you tomorrow morning. Or even late tonight."

"What?" Potts sounded as if he had swallowed his spearmint. "Say, if you're holding out on me one little eenyweeny drop of dope, I'll hang ya as an accomplice before and after the fact."

"I'm not holding out a thing."

"Charlie get in touch with ya?"

"Yes."

"Where are ya going to see him?"

Bill hung up softly.

"Are the police trying to find Charlie Beach?" Ruth asked.

"Yes. I'm going to see him tonight."

Ruth shuddered slightly. "Charlie Beach couldn't have done it. He's a little cracked, that's true, but he couldn't—he wouldn't dare."

"That's what I think."

"The police'll never give him a chance. They'll take advantage of him and force him into saying all kinds of crazy things. It'll be terrible for him. If you can help him, you must."

Bill sighed. "Maybe. If he's got any kind of an alibi."

The phone rang again. It was for Ruth, and Bill left the outer office for his own.

At three o'clock, Bill met Sue Huxley in front of the City Hall. Sue was amazingly bright looking for having been flooded through the night before with Potts' Irish.

"Before we go up to the Hall of Records," Bill suggested amiably, "let's you and I stop in and see a friend of mine."

"Who?"

Bill squinted his eyes mysteriously. "Just a friend."

They stopped in front of a clerk in the Marriage Bureau.

"I want a marriage license," Bill said.

"Who are you going to marry?" asked Sue.

"You."

"Why?"

Bill shrugged. "I always say it's good for heartburn."

"Why not try bicarbonate of soda?"

"What's the name of the man?" the clerk asked sourly.

"William Benedict."

"And the bride?"

"Susan Ann Huxley," said Bill. Sue kept quiet.

The clerk got their ages and addresses and their parents' names. When it came to signing, Sue inquired from the clerk whether she had to get married once she put her name to the application.

"Lady," said the man, "you was your own boss before, and you can be your own boss yet. This paper—" he waved the license indifferently, "don't mean a thing. The city requires it, that's all. But as far as the city's consoined you can use it to make out your next week's laundry list."

"Thanks for the suggestion." She signed it. "I feel peculiarly passive this morning."

"Never can tell," Bill said on their way up to the Hall of Records. "It might come in handy one of these days. We'll be alone in your apartment or mine, and I'll have your gin rickey nicely doped up. 'Will you marry me?' I'll say. And you'll be too cat-eyed to deny me the divine right of kings. So you'll say, 'Yes.' And if I have to wait to get a license the next day, you'll change your mind. This way, we can marry right off, then and there."

"You think of everything," Sue said, with a touch of admiration in her voice.

They spent the rest of the afternoon sniffing through dusty cards and ledgers and lists. "There are almost as many Murrays in New York as Cohns and Smiths," Bill said at six o'clock.

"Too many Murrays," Sue whispered wearily. "Let's quit."

"Coward!" An hour later Bill clapped his hands with a loud bang. "Let's eat."

Bill pulled Sue to a Russian restaurant near Park Row and they had onion-cakes and sour cream.

Boley gulped down three straight double Scotches at the bar of his hotel. Then he went upstairs to get his key to the baggage room. When he got inside the room he made sure he was alone and opened a big packing case with his name stenciled on it. Near the bottom, his fingers gripped the cool barrel of an old service revolver. He slipped it into his pocket, wheeled the packing case back into place, and went down to the bar again for another double Scotch.

He took a cab for Washington Square; then walked west. It was near suppertime. The playgrounds were empty. The lights of the apartment houses bordering the Square were yellow patches against the blue evening sky. Boley felt chilly. He put up his coat collar. Once or twice he fingered the revolver in his pocket.

On Bleecker Street, he stopped in front of an old-law tenement house, looked up and down the street, and hurriedly climbed the stone steps. He walked up five flights. At the top landing, he paused to catch his breath. There was a door at the end of the dark, dirty hall. He knocked and called out softly, "Charlie . . . Charlie Beach." There was no answer. He took a key out of his pocket.

The room was empty and cold. The one window was open. Boley shivered and closed it. The only furnishings in the room were a small cot under the window, a scarred kitchen table, and a stool. Boley lit a match and looked around. He muttered something. A closet in a corner caught his attention. He strode toward it impatiently. It was empty. The match flickered out. He lit another. Then he noticed something he had overlooked before. On the table was an old cigarette carton filled with torn scraps of paper. He picked up some of the pieces. There was writing on them. He lit another match. It was unsteady in his trembling hands. He read the writing. . . .

Boley cursed softly, his face flushing in the half-light. He stuck the scraps of paper in his pocket and blew out his match. Cautiously, he opened the door to the hall a few inches. He waited. No one was coming up or down. He stepped out quickly.

"Hello."

Boley said, "Hello."

"Find the place okay?"

"Yeah."

"Did the key work?"

Boley nodded. The man opposite smiled in a satisfied way. They were sitting at a table in a chophouse near the Bowery.

"You got to do another job for me, Freddie," Boley said.

Freddie leaned forward and dashed some salt into his beer. He was a man in his fifties with a round, pale face and a thin nose he kept pulling. He spoke with a slight Limehouse accent.

"I'm listenin'."

Boley took the scraps out of his pocket, glanced through them, and shoved one across the table. Freddie read it.

"Hell. This is a street corner, man."

"I know."

"What erbout it?"

"The guy you found for me beat it."

"That ain't up to me."

"I know it ain't."

"No clothes or things?"

"No books. That guy can go without pants, but not without books."

"A screwy nut, eh?"

"Yeah."

Freddie pointed to the slip of paper. "He leave these?"

"Yeah. I figure he wrote a letter to someone saying to meet him. Probably tore up a couple of sheets of paper before he was satisfied. I know who he's going to meet, I know where, and I know it's going to be at midnight tonight."

"What do you want I should do?"

Boley finished his beer and signaled to a waiter. "Get there ten minutes ahead of time. Pick this guy up."

"Then what?"

Boley tapped softly on the table. "He's going to try to speak to someone." He paused. "I don't want him to."

Freddie whistled low. "Snatch?"

The big Irishman lowered his eyes and looked off in a corner. "I don't want him ever to see that guy or anyone else." The waiter came over. "Two more beers. Spike mine with gin."

Freddie pulled at his nose. "You're on the wrong horse, Mister."

"Scared?"

"These days, it ain't easy."

"Two grand."

"Not for ten."

"Know anyone else interested?"

Freddie ran a long finger across his fat face. He shook his head. "Not in New York."

"Where?"

"Minneapolis."

"Tonight, it's got to be."

Freddie considered. "For ten grand, I'd like to oblige."

"I'll make it ten."

The waiter brought the beer. Boley's hand trembled as he brought the glass to his mouth.

Freddie sighed. "If you're so hot about it, why don't you do it yourself?"

Boley spilled some beer on his fingers. Hurriedly, he pulled a handkerchief out of his breast-pocket and wiped them.

"Scared?"

Boley took a deep breath. "No."

"Okay." Freddie pushed his chair back from the table and got up. "I'll be watchin' the papers."

After dinner, Sue and Bill took a bus ride up Fifth Avenue. The night was pleasantly warm for October, and they could sit up on top.

"Well, we wasted a whole afternoon . . . and what did we get?" Sue inquired oratorically. "A lot of Murrays and some sour cream."

"I got a marriage license."

Sue permitted her head to fall on Bill's shoulder by degrees. At 110th Street, they fell asleep. At 168th Street and Broadway, the conductor woke them up for their return fares.

A little later Bill pointed to the Hudson gleaming below them. "Look, darling. Niagara Falls."

Sue yawned unromantically. "Turn over," she said. "Your cold feet are killing me."

"Say, conductor," Bill called out. "What time is it?"

"Nine-thirty."

"Wake me at ten, will you?"

The conductor nodded and rubbed his name-plate wonderingly. "Nuts, Greenwich Village nuts." He went below.

At ten o'clock, they were at 72nd Street. Bill glanced at his Ingersoll just as the conductor climbed to the top to wake him.

"Huxley," Bill nudged her. "Huxley, I've got to leave you now."

Sue opened her eyes slowly. "What?"

"I've got to beat it. I'm late."

"Jilted at Niagara Falls, oh my God!"

"Finish out the ride yourself. I've paid for the tickets. The conductor'll see you home. Won't you, Mr. Leary?" Bill saw the name-plate clearly in a passing lamp.

"Where does the Missus get off?"

"Forty-fourth Street."

"I'll take care of it for ye."

Bill kissed Sue on her lips and darted down the steps.

Bill waved to her and hopped into a cab. "Forty-fifth and Broadway, brother," Bill said.

Bill walked toward Shubert's Alley from Broadway. It was a quarter to eleven. None of the audiences had been let out yet. Groups of chauffeurs stood chatting in the warm squares of golden light thrown on the sidewalk from the lobbies. Ranked along the curb from Broadway to Eighth Avenue were fancy limousines reflecting with their high polish the electric signs over the theaters. Taxis filled the middle of the street like a line of purring yellow cats ready to pounce. And alongside each cab with a hand on the door-handle was a little Dead End kid prepared, for a consideration, to risk life and limb to open the door for customers.

The street was relatively quiet; the cars and taxis were at a standstill. The pools of light in front of each theater—the Booth, the Plymouth, the John Golden, the Majestic, the Music Box— were like the camp fires of African explorers keeping away, by their flames, a ring of tigers and lions and hyenas menacingly eager to jump.

Bill stood a little way in the Alley next to the Booth. It was dark at his end except for the red exit lights. He lit a cigarette and waited. His eyes moved unceasingly over the length of the Alley and up and down 45th Street. Once or twice he crossed over to 44th Street. Charlie might be coming from downtown.

At a few minutes before eleven, the street became alive with the first of the departing audiences. Then gradually came a wave of movement and noise. Hackies raced their motors, chauffeurs turned on the ignition of their limousines. Up from Broadway trotted a half dozen newsboys with tomorrow's paper.

The chatter and noise and movement increased. The John Golden's doors were opened, then the Booth's and from the innards of the theater came the last applause.

The little area around the end of Shubert's Alley became a whirlpool of people and cries and horns honking and kids yelling, "Here's your taxi. . . . Here's your taxi. . . ." And the newsboys with their sports final and a new European crisis . . . and dowagers calling to each other . . . and laughter and pushing and yelling.

"Hello . . ."

Bill suddenly found himself confronted by Charlie. "Where the hell did you come from?"

Charlie made a move with his thin hand. "What's the diff?"

The boy's eyes seemed to hang from his head by wire strings. They snapped from one side of his head to the other, constantly moving, constantly afraid. His face was pale. He kept biting his lips until the tips of his teeth were stained with blood.

He grabbed Bill's arm. "Come on, let's get out of here."

"What's up?" They started to push their way through the crowds in front of the Booth.

"I got to talk to you!" The words came with desperate rapidity. The boy was panting. "You didn't tell anybody, did you?"

"No," Bill almost got knocked off his feet by a stout gentleman in evening clothes who was making a dash for a car at the curb. He felt Charlie's fingers lose their grip on his arm.

The taxis screamed for fares; the limousines honked their way through; the street kids yelled . . . and men and women shoved and pushed each other—politely, of course—but with determination.

Bill turned around. He was completely engulfed by the crowd. He lost sight of Charlie. Then he saw him a couple of feet away struggling to get to him. The boy, his eyes balls of fear, roughly elbowed his way through some chattering women. He must have hurt one of the women. She turned to him to protest. A car backfired loudly. At that moment, Charlie stiffened up and turned his head wildly from side to side.

"Bill!" Then he folded up and fell to the sidewalk.

Bill ran to him. A woman screamed, "Someone's fainted! Get a doctor!" A large pond of blood surrounded Charlie. It was coming out of a hole in his back. Bill turned him over and looked at the boy's anguished face. He was dead.

"Get back!" Bill ordered the well-dressed women and men who were trying to push their way past. Charlie's blood lapped at the toes of their evening shoes; they stepped away hastily.

"Someone get a cop!"

A doorman whistled three hysterical times; from Broadway came an answer. A couple of cops ran up.

Bill pointed to Charlie's body. "Take him away," he said huskily. "And, for God's sakes, call Lieutenant Potts."

"You come along with us, guy," one of the cops said.

"Sure, just a minute." He walked unsteadily into the Alley back where it was dark . . . and got sick.

CHAPTER XIII
"A 21 JEWEL DOPE"

"Ya sure do get around," Potts said with a chuckle that had no humor in it. "Is this what ya meant when ya said on the phone you'd have something to tell me about Charlie Beach tonight?"

Bill was silent. He took a long pull at his drink and closed his eyes. He tried to recall the faces of all the people who had passed him on his way from the Alley to where he had stopped to wait for Charlie.

"Leo Murray gets killed in your room. Charlie Beach gets shot while walking with you. Hell, you're just a good-luck sign, that's all." The huge detective shuddered. "From now on, my friend, when we do any talking it'll be in a police station."

Bill Benedict said: "Nuts."

The phone rang. Potts answered. "Yeah. . . . Uh uh. . . . No. . . . Okay." He hung up; then dialed. "Lieutenant Potts speaking. Send out word to all precincts and radio cars to be on the lookout for a thirty-eight service type. Check up on all stores that handle them. Send in a report on all purchasers of guns within the last year. . . . How close do you figure assailant was? Under six feet, eh? . . . Okay."

He turned to Benedict, his large head drooping heavily on his chest. "Ya heard what I said—" He nodded to the phone.

"A service revolver," Bill mused. "There's lots of 'em around, eh Potts?"

"Yeah—what about it?"

"Nothing." Bill's eyes narrowed.

"You were right alongside when he got it. Didn't ya see nobody?"

Bill shook his head.

"Was it you?"

Bill smiled bitterly. "Nope."

"Got anything that proves ya didn't?"

"Got anything that proves I did?"

Potts moved out of his chair and walked across the room. He kept shaking his head from side to side like a St. Bernard getting rid of water.

He said finally: "Well . . . that gets rid of Charlie Beach."

"Yeah. Where's that inspiration you were talking about?"

Potts glared at him glumly.

"We've got to assume that Charlie Beach had something on Leo Murray's murderer which he was going to tell me tonight. So Charlie was wiped out."

"That's simple. What else?"

Bill slowly opened a pack of cigarettes. "The murderer doesn't know that Charlie didn't get a chance to say anything."

"He only hopes."

"So maybe I'm next on the list."

"Maybe. . . ."

"Maybe, hell! I've got to find that guy before he finds me."

"Where are ya going to look?"

Bill slumped in his chair. "I wish you were Perry Mason or Philo Vance or Charlie Chan or someone, and not a—"

"Don't say it," said Potts evenly. "Anybody know you was going to meet Charlie Beach tonight?"

"No . . . yes."

"Who?"

"Ruth Murray."

"Leo's sister, eh." Potts reached for a phone.

"She didn't know where or when."

"She could've followed ya."

Bill smiled. "All day? I was on the empty top of a Fifth Avenue Bus from eight o'clock to ten."

"Alone?"

"With Sue Huxley. She'll verify no one was following us; no one could."

Potts moved his hand away from the phone. "Nick Finley?"

"He's among the starters."

"Don't let his socking ya bias ya."

"No law against socking me, eh?"

"You get rewards."

"Comrade," said Bill.

"Frank Boley is another. I had him tailed until my man got acute alcoholism. There's Ricky Linton and Alice Lawrence and Steve Levy and MacMonnies."

"And Billy Rose and Mayor La Guardia and Gypsy Rose Lee and Samuel Untermyer."

Bill's eyes suddenly closed.

"What's the matter, feeling faint?"

Suddenly, Bill arose and reached for his topcoat. "Through with me?"

The detective raised his shaggy eyebrows. "Where're ya going?"

"Home."

"What for?"

"To sleep. I'm tired."

"Ain't ya scared to go alone?"

Bill frowned. "Make me a special deputy and give me a gun."

"I'll put a man tailing ya. That'll do it."

Bill's face stiffened. "No. I sleep alone."

"Let me in on it."

"Good night, Mr. Potts."

"Okay," said Potts. "Here." He stamped a piece of paper with his signature and pulled a gun and a Bible out of his drawer. "This isn't strictly the McCoy but it'll do."

Bill mumbled something. Potts gave him the revolver. "Know how to use this?"

"I never fired one in my life," Bill said sarcastically.

Bill got out of his cab a block away from Nick Finley's house. He made sure that he wasn't being followed and walked the rest of the way. Finley opened the door cautiously.

"Oh . . . it's you," he said irritably.

"Who'd you think it was—the cops?" Bill asked.

Finley locked and bolted the door. "Have a drink?" Bill nodded. The producer was dressed in a lounging gown that was a cross between a shamrock green and a Battery harbor-blue. He looked squatter than usual and his round face was deflated into shadowy hollows and lines.

"Scotch or rye?" Finley asked, turning to Bill.

"Bourbon and water. I feel a cold coming on."

Finley brought over a bottle of Bourbon and a silver water bottle. "Help yourself."

"What's the matter, Nick? You look terrible."

Nick avoided the question. "What kept you so long?"

"Kept me?"

"I been ringing you at the Chicopee since six o'clock. It was important. What the hell d'ya think I'm paying you three hundred a week for?"

Bill poured the Bourbon into a glass. "What did you want, Nick?"

"I'm in a helluva fix. You got to help me."

"Okay." Bill took his glass in hand and walked over to the French windows overlooking Central Park.

"Goddamn you! Look at me when I talk to you!"

Bill turned to Nick, his lips curling slowly in a smile. "I'm looking."

The producer drew a deep breath as if his outburst had been too much for him.

"I'm being taken over, Bill. Someone's got a finger on me. I'm goin' nuts!"

"For God's sake, Nick, what's happened?"

"I'm being blackmailed!"

Bill laughed out loud.

"What's so funny?" Finley shouted, his face flushed with anger.

"I'm sorry, Nick." Bill's face straightened. He took a sip of his Bourbon solemnly. "Who is it?"

"I been a damn' fool, Bill. I can talk straight from the shoulder to you. I was so sore at Leo, I'd've done anything I could to break him up so I hired a guy to stink-bomb the Arcadia opening night." Finley paused and squirmed under Bill's direct stare.

"You hired a guy to do that?" Bill's tone carried his apparent incredulity. "Jesus, I can't believe it."

Finley moaned. "So help me. I'm a fool."

"I'll say you are. Who is the guy?"

"Some rat named Laney. He wants ten thousand dollars from me. He threatens to tell the cops." The Irishman rocked on the couch and started to keen. "It's worse than that. He's the guy I was walking with in the park the time Leo was killed. He says he'll go to the cops and say I threatened to kill Leo. . . . Something's gotta be done, Bill. The guy'll blast me over the front pages and I'll be blown up higher'n a kite. I'll get kicked out of the Managers' Association. I won't be able to produce. There'll be a scandal. I'll be ruined!"

Bill put his glass down. "Is that all to the story?"

"So help me, Bill." Finley's face was covered with tiny drops of perspiration, and he kept tapping his fingers together nervously. "Bill, you gotta get me out of this."

"What do you want me to do?"

"Go down and see this guy. Talk hard-boiled to 'im. You used to be a dick. You know how to handle mugs. I'll give a grand if you get rid of 'im. He lives at 310 West 20th Street."

Bill's lips pressed tightly together. He looked sharply at Finley. "No homicide for me."

"I'm not askin' anything like that, Bill. I wouldn't think of it." Finley rose and walked over to Bill. He looked at him pleadingly. "All I'm asking is to try. It don't hurt. Maybe ya can scare 'im off. Do you know the guy? Did you ever hear of 'im?"

Bill nodded. "I got enough on the screwball to send him away for twenty years."

The Irishman smiled happily. "There you are You can do it. It's a grand for you!"

Bill thought a minute and drained his glass. "Okay, Nick. Only it'll cost you five grand."

Finley whistled.

"Just half, Nick. Laney wants ten. You give me five. That's settling for fifty cents on a dollar."

"Okay, I'll do it."

Bill took a quick look at his watch. It was eleven-forty. He said:

"Happy Vorhaus is still at his office. Write out a note to him to give me five thousand dollars in cash."

Finley opened his eyes wide. "You have to have the dough now?"

"Yep."

"Ya trust me, don't ya?" Finley was hurt.

"Sure, I trust you, Nick. But I do business this way. It's a principle with me. Pay on acceptance."

"But what if this Laney guy won't scare?"

"I'll return forty-five hundred. The other five's a service charge."

Nick hesitated a long time; then he moved slowly toward his desk and pulled out a checkbook. He wrote one and handed it to Bill.

"Thanks," said Bill. "Where's your gun, Nick? I may need it. No rough stuff, I assure you. Just to make it look real."

Nick paled. "No, ya don't, Bill! I ain't giving you the gun. Anything happen, it'll be traced to me. You do this on your own."

"You still got it?"

Nick smiled craftily. "Sure."

"Won't you give it to me?"

"No, sir!" Finley was determined. Bill shrugged and got his hat.

"Another drink before you go, Bill?" Nick asked hospitably.

"No. . . . By the way, Nick," Bill said as he stood at the door, "Charlie Beach was murdered an hour or so ago. He was killed by a service-type revolver."

The squat man began to tremble. His haggard face flushed, then blanched. "Charlie!"

"Yeah."

Finley began to knit his hands nervously. "This is terrible," he moaned.

"Yeah . . . I figured that's what you'd think," Bill said sourly as he closed the door and walked down the hall toward the elevator.

Nick waited until he heard the elevator descend. He walked to the porch outside his window and looked over. In a few minutes, he saw Bill emerge from the apartment house door and get into a taxicab. Then he went back into his living room to the phone and dialed a Chelsea number.

"Hello . . . Call Jock Laney to the phone. . . . Thanks. . . . Laney? Nick Finley speaking. . . . Yeah. . . . I made up my mind to come through. I'm sending down a friend of mine. He's got the ten grand with him. . . . Yeah, I said ten grand. I told 'im to give it you. . . . And that's all you get from me. Not a cent more. Okay. . . . Good night."

Nick hung up. He nodded smugly. "A goddamn little Napoleon, that's what I am," he muttered and went over and poured himself a drink.

Bill took the cab to Vorhaus' and cashed Nick's check. He put the five one-thousand dollar bills in an envelope and addressed it to William Benedict, Chicopee Hotel, New York, N. Y. He mailed it and took a cab downtown to 20th Street.

Laney lived on a street in the heart of Chelsea, that footsore district in New York where rent is cheap and where there are more infant deaths than anywhere else in the city. Twentieth Street is one of the quietest of the Chelsea streets. Between 8th and 9th Avenues, it contains a fine church, a seminary and a lawn, a machine shop turned into an amateur theater, a fire house, a public school, three Italian stores, three Irish stores, countless boarding houses and one elevator apartment. From six in the morning until one in the morning the street is always crowded with kids. From one A. M. until six it's as empty as a vacuum except when someone commits murder or suicide. When Bill drove up to 310, the apartment house, it was one in the morning.

If Laney was surprised to see Bill he didn't show it. He asked him to sit down and pushed over a half-empty bottle of rye.

"Drink?"

"Got any Bourbon?"

"Nope."

"I'll take rye." Bill filled his own glass and gulped the raw stuff down. He coughed.

"I got the money for you, Laney," Bill said after a while.

Laney nodded.

"Who killed Murray?"

Laney's eyes squinted in surprise. Bill repeated the question. Laney kept quiet. Bill arose abruptly.

"Where ya goin', Benny?"

"Home."

"What for?" Laney shifted in his chair and reached for the bottle.

"I don't have time to waste, Laney. You tell me who murdered Leo, I give you five grand."

"Ya just gonna give me *five* grand, eh?"

Bill smiled. "Sure. That's what we agreed."

The gangster rubbed fingers across his chin. He rose from the chair and walked over to the window. He lifted the shade a trifle, then let it fall flapping back.

"Well?" asked Bill.

Laney smiled and showed his teeth. He made a gesture with his hand. "Why do you want to double-cross me, Benny?"

Bill laughed and lit a cigarette but he kept his eyes on Laney's right hand.

"Benny, you're a dope. I t'ought you was smart but you're a dope anyway. I know Finley sent ya down here with ten grand—not five. To buy me off, see? Not to find out what I know about the Murray knifer."

"Finley call you?"

"Ya think he's a dope like you?"

"Laney, I'm going to ask you a question," Bill said moving slightly toward Laney's right. "Did you kill Charlie Beach with your own gun or with Finley's service revolver?"

Again, Laney's eyes squinted in surprise. "Anudder guy get his, eh?"

Bill nodded. "How'd you do it—and with what?"

"With nothin'. I didn't know this Beach guy. And I didn't know Murray."

"What do you know about Finley?"

"That he gave ya ten grand to give me." Laney stepped behind his chair and ran his fingers tentatively along the top.

"Why?"

"Because he loves me. Now gimme the ten."

Bill grinned. "One minute, Laney. If your sense of morals pro-hibits you from squealing on Mr. Finley, permit me to outline the situation. You don't have to say yes or no. Nick Finley hired you to kill Murray. You did. You got paid for it. Now, you're black-mailing him for more. Some way or another, Charlie Beach knew about it. You had to get rid of him. You found out that he was going to meet me tonight at eleven o'clock at Shubert's Alley. I don't know how you found out, but you did. You killed him with a .38 service-type revolver. The cops know that already. But what they don't know is that I saw a rod like that up in Finley's apart-ment. I asked him for it tonight. He didn't have it. My guess is it's here. What do you say, Laney?"

Laney laughed heartily. "You're a dope, Benny. A 21 jewel dope."

Bill looked at him, puzzled. "What's wrong in the picture?"

"Murray was knocked over at eight o'clock. At eight, I was walkin' with Finley—and Finley was walkin' with me. In Central Park by the zoo, near the monkeys like you."

"You alibi each other—so what?"

Laney shook his head pityingly. "And at eleven ternight, I got an alibi not even you can break. Ya know?—at eleven—when I'm supposed to be slippin' it to this Beach guy?"

Bill swallowed painfully. "What's your alibi?"

Laney shoved a piece of paper in his face. "A ticket for passing a red light. Got at 23rd Street. The time is marked on it. Now, you dumb sonuvabitch, gimme my ten grand and get the hell outta here."

"I don't have the money."

Laney's face wrinkled tensely.

"I left it home," Bill said, watching Laney's right hand. Then something terrific hit him. His head was jerked back and he tried to duck away. Laney's left hand held the butt end of a gun. He smashed into Bill's face a second time. Bill fell to the floor. Laney made sure and slammed the gun down on the top of his head. He turned Bill over on his back. Bill was breathing—and that's all.

Laney dug quickly through Bill's pockets. There was no money in them. He ran downstairs to a pay station telephone and called Nick Finley. No one answered.

At about two o'clock in the morning, Sue got tired of waiting up for Bill to come home. She went downstairs to get a morning paper and a package of cigarettes. The headlines made her forget the cigarettes.

CHARLIE BEACH, MURRAY MURDER
SUSPECT KILLED
THEATER CROWD HYSTERICAL AS
ASSAILANT ESCAPES

Charlie Beach, 34, well-known play director, was mysteriously shot and killed in front of the Booth Theater, 45th Street West of Broadway, as the audience was leaving the theater.... Lieutenant Potts in charge of the Murray case revealed that Beach had been one of the suspects in the unsolved murder of Leo Murray, noted producer, who was stabbed three nights ago.... With Beach at the time was William Benedict, press-agent of the late Leo Murray, and well-known Broadwayite. Benedict was arrested on the spot by Traffic Patrolman Nealy who . . .

Sue borrowed five dollars from the night clerk and hopped into a cab for the 52nd Street police station. At the station she brushed aside a couple of drunks and went up to the sergeant's desk.

"Where's Bill Benedict?"

"Who?"

"Benedict, Benedict, the man arrested on the Beach murder."

The sergeant shook his bald head. "No arrests were made."

"Here!" She shoved the paper under his nose.

He read it. "Nope. You can't believe what you read in the papers."

Sue was relieved. "I ought to have known that. I write for them."

"It makes no difference to me, lady," the cop said.

"Is Lieutenant Potts here?"

"Nope."

"Where is he?"

"Home."

"What's he doing at home?"

The sergeant patted his dome resentfully. "Now, lady, can't a cop have a private life?"

"When did Benedict leave here?"

"A couple of hours ago."

Sue bit her nail nervously. "He ought to have been back to the hotel by this time."

"Are you the wife?"

"No," said Sue smartly and walked out. She took a cab to Potts' hotel. The night clerk refused any information.

"It's a matter of life or death," said Sue.

"Oh yeah?"

"Yes, life or death."

"I'll ring him. Hello, Lieutenant Potts? . . . Sorry, sir, but there's a lady here who says it's a matter of— Yes, how did you know, sir? One minute, please." The clerk handed Sue the phone. "He says that he knows it's a matter of life and death. It always is."

Sue spoke quickly. "This is Susan Huxley. Remember me? Yes. . . . I'll come right up." She gave the clerk a snooty fare-thee-well and skipped over to the elevator.

Hake Potts met her at the door in a beige dressing gown that looked like something a Scotchman had given to the Salvation Army at the time of the San Francisco earthquake.

Potts shoved a chair forward. "Your boy been killed or somethin'?"

"I don't know, Lieutenant. Maybe."

"What's up?"

"He's not home."

"Should he be?"

Sue shrugged. "I don't know."

"Did you think you'd find him under my bed?"

Sue was silent.

"Or did ya come to have a crystal-gazing party with me just because you're lonely?"

"But it's almost three o'clock."

"I know just what ya mean," said Potts dryly. "Well. . . ?"

Sue rose and started for the door. "I'm sorry, Mr. Potts. He hasn't come back to the hotel, and I read that Charlie Beach was murdered and Bill was arrested . . . and I was worried."

Potts sighed. "Beach was bumped off, Bill wasn't arrested, and you've no reason to be worried. Go home and get some sleep. I need it too." He watched her a moment and smiled. "I'll tell Bill ya were all hot and bothered about him."

"Don't!"

"So I won't tell him," said Potts, still smiling.

"Good night."

Sue went back to her hotel, read a detective story for a while, and fell asleep.

When Bill came to, he saw, as if in a fog, the tight, dark, angry face of Laney in front of him. Laney saw his eyes opening and pulled him to his feet. Bill wavered unsteadily and wiped the blood from his mouth.

"Listen, Benny—" Laney's voice was even. "Finley swears he gave ya ten grand. Where is it?"

Bill swayed and didn't answer.

"Okay, Benny." Laney smashed his fist against Bill's eye, knocking him down. He threw some whisky in his face and picked him up.

"Where's the dough?"

Bill tried to open his lips and yell. Before he had a chance, Laney knocked him down again.

"Ya gonna tell me?" Laney snarled. Bill shook his head. Laney kicked him in the stomach. Bill dropped like a sack of potatoes. Laney left the room and went downstairs to call Finley for the tenth time.

Bill opened his one good eye and turned it slowly around the room. He saw that he was alone. He caught a leg of a table and pulled himself painfully to his feet. Laney was still downstairs.

Bill moved slowly to the door. He tried it and found it locked. Then he dropped to his knees out of weakness and crawled to the window at the far end of the room. He looked out. The street was empty. He heard Laney's footsteps coming up the stairs. Bill stood up as quickly as he could and remained standing in front of the window. Laney entered.

"Stick 'em up and gimme your gun, Laney," Bill said hoarsely, faking with his pipe. Laney turned quickly and reached in his pocket. A revolver gleamed in the half-light. Bill swayed. Laney's gun snorted. Bill fell. The window-glass behind him crashed into the street below. Instantly, with the sound of the gun and crashing glass, there came excited yelling of people in adjoining houses and apartments. From Seventh Avenue, Bill heard a police-car siren. He couldn't see Laney and he dared not make a move, but he could hear Laney shuffle some clothes together and snap down a valise. The door slammed and Laney's steps rang hurriedly down the stairs.

CHAPTER XIV
"F.D.R. PLANS CRUISE."

Next morning Bill succeeded in persuading a skeptical desk sergeant to call Lieutenant Potts before being sent over to the Magistrate's Court.

When Potts arrived, Bill was pacing his cell with a splitting headache. He greeted the detective indignantly. "You have the dumbest police department in America."

"What happened?" Potts asked, amused. "Arrested for jaywalking?"

"Jaywalking, hell! For firing a gun and being drunk."

Potts stopped chewing and grinned.

"Stop thinking up a wisecrack and get your men busy picking up a mug named Jock Laney, alias Lawrence, alias M'Carey—"

Potts became serious.

"Jock Laney in town?"

"Yes! Pick 'im up in a hurry. I think he can tell us something about the Murray case."

"When did ya see him?"

"Last night."

"This is a helluva time to let me know."

Bill sat down on a stool in disgust. "I tried to explain to your goddamn dumb cops all night, but you think they listen? I'm half dead trying to explain."

Potts' face reddened and he yelled some orders to the sergeant.

"Now, Bill, tell me all about it."

Bill groaned. "I'm sick. Get me a doctor. My head feels like a rubber balloon. Until I feel better, I'm not talking."

A little while later, a police surgeon came in. He ordered some ice-bags. Bill had escaped serious injury. "Although," said the surgeon, "you come mighty close to a class B concussion. You really got hit."

Potts insisted that Bill explain before he let him go home. "Laney had offered to tell me who the murderer is for five thousand dollars. And when I went to see him to get the dope, he tried to double-cross me and get the five grand without spilling. I didn't like it so I told him to go to hell. As a result, I got beat up. And that's all I know."

Potts looked at him suspiciously. "You're a liar, Bill."

Bill shrugged his shoulders. "That's all I know."

"You mean, that's all ya want me to know."

"Have it your way, Potts. I want to go home."

The detective chewed thoughtfully. "Bill," he said finally, "I'm gonna pick up this Laney boy. If he lets on that you know more'n ya say, you're never gonna get your agency license back."

Bill sighed. "Get me a cab, will ya? I'm weary."

Back in his hotel room, after several hours of ice-bags, Bill told the complete story to Sue. "I figured that the only way I could get out was to force Laney to make a helluva lot of noise. I took a chance on falling to the floor a split-second before he shot. It worked. He broke the window and the cops came. He got cold feet and ran away."

Before Sue had a chance to question him there was a knock at the door.

"Come."

Potts entered.

"Ah—" said Sue hastily. "The man with the beige pajamas."

"Can't find Laney," Potts announced gloomily.

Bill sat up in bed. "Did they find the gun that killed Charlie?"

Potts shook his head. He walked over to the bed where Bill lay, his head encased in ice-bags.

"Did ya change your mind about tellin' me the whole Laney story? Who else was mixed up in it?"

There was a sudden silence in the room. Bill stared unseeing up to the ceiling, Potts chewed his gum with a squishy sound, and Sue gazed thoughtfully at the spiraling smoke from her cigarette.

Finally from Bill came a low muttering, "MacMonnies, Ricky Linton, Alice Lawrence, Ruth Murray, Frank Boley, Nick Finley, MacMonnies, Ricky Linton, Alice Lawrence, Frank Boley, Nick Finley, Frank Boley, Ruth Murray, Alice Lawrence, Ricky Linton, MacMonnies, Ricky—"

"For Chrissakes, shut up!" Potts yelled.

"I'm only listing the suspects."

Potts glared at Bill. "Are you trying to ding-dong me?"

"I wouldn't think of it."

"This is the lousiest case I ever been on. You work—a guy ya trust lies to ya, people get killed—and there's nothing new."

"Why not?" Sue asked. "Huh? Why not?"

"Because, there's nothin' new."

"How do you know?"

"Listen, you two little second-string dicks. Off and on I had a man on the tail of every suspect in this case. I got daily reports. . . . So what? So the whole goddamned bunch of 'em are livin' normal lives."

"Could I take a look at those reports?" Bill asked suddenly.

"Sure. What are you going to do, Ellery Queen 'em?"

"A little logic wouldn't hurt." He stepped out of bed and walked up and down the hotel room trailing his blanket around him.

"Sit down, Indian," said Sue. "You'll catch a cold on top of whatever you've got now."

"Leo is knifed by a Mr. X. From the angle of the wound, etc., it is deduced that the murderer was taller than the victim, and pretty strong. The time of death is set between eight and eight-thirty. All possible suspects have alibis or are in places where no alibi is possible. A telegram is sent to the sister of the dead man warning her to sell her interest in his show or else. . . . And Charlie Beach, whom the Law suspects as the murderer, asks to see me and is killed before he has a chance. And, lastly, a mug who says he knows who killed Murray tries to kill me. What does that all add up to?"

"Two murders and a pretty beating-up for Bill Benedict," Sue said half-heartedly.

"Further and further. Mr. X who murdered Leo Murray also sent the telegram to Murray's sister and murdered Charlie Beach."

He stopped short. "Potts, did you check up on everybody *in re* Charlie's murder?"

Potts said wearily: "They have alibis that can't be broken. Like the last time. The only man I haven't talked to is Laney."

"Bill," Sue said. "Listening to you rant I must conclude that a logician is a dope who sits in a loge. Now watch a big leaguer at work. If the Medical Examiner is correct that the blow must have come from a taller man, then all you have to do is to narrow down your list of possibilities to tall, strong men." She waved her hands triumphantly. "And that let's *me* out."

"It let's everybody out but Ricky Linton, Frank Boley, and MacMonnies," said Bill.

Someone rapped at the door.

"Answer it, Sue," said Bill, bouncing back into bed.

"Sure, what'd it say?"

Bill threw a pillow at her as Potts opened the door. The pillow missed Sue and halted on a bellhop's face.

"The guest is always right at the Chicopee," the boy said handing Potts an envelope. "For Christy Mathewson over there."

"I'll see you later, fellow," Bill said. The boy left the room.

Bill opened the envelope. A newspaper clipping fell out. He read it and handed it to Potts. Sue looked over his shoulder.

F.D.R. PLANS CRUISE
TO CURE HIS COLD

Washington. Sept. 24 (UP)—President Roosevelt will spend the week end aboard the yacht Potomac if the crisis in Europe permits.

He will seek a salt air cure for a head cold that has kept him confined most of the week to his second floor study. The cold forced him to cancel all but the most important engagements. Necessary appointments were kept in his study instead of in the executive offices.

He will leave tomorrow evening, it was reported.

"Some kind of code," Sue said.

"I didn't think Frank was inviting me to go along with him."

"Let me have it," Potts ordered. He sat down at a desk and copied off the underlined letters. Bill and Sue watched him intently.

P-l-e-a-s-e-d-o-n-o-t-t-r-y-t-o-f-i-n-d-m-e

"Please do not try to find me," Potts muttered.

Bill walked across the room to close the window.

"Bill!" Sue screamed. "Get away from there! A man gets a warning note and he walks in front of an open window."

Potts examined the envelope. "Mailed at the Hudson Terminal Post Office."

Bill grabbed the clipping from Potts' hand. "The clipping's from the *New York Post*."

Potts chewed rapidly and wet his lips like a fire horse hearing the alarm. Then he said suddenly, "Miss Huxley, don't let him get out of this room until I say so. Otherwise, I don't take no responsibility."

"What are you going to do about the note?" Bill asked.

Potts was exalted by some kind of inner excitement. He said: "Today's Wednesday. Give me a week."

"What then?"

"I'm gonna have the Murray murderer."

"Another hunch?" Bill asked slyly. "Like on Charlie Beach?"

Potts walked to the door like a man with a champagne drunk. "I can't be wrong twice," he said airily. "And, by the way, my orders is that *you* stay put until I tell ya otherwise."

CHAPTER XV
LITTLE MAN, WHAT NOW?

"There are three things," said Bill, later in the day, in between gulps of beer, "that worry me."

"Me, you, and what else?" Sue asked.

"The knife thrust, the bill for toys which came to Leo Murray, and his plans for an immediate exodus to London." Bill walked over to his bureau and took out a long champagne swizzle stick that he had swiped from a Paris bar.

"We'll start with the knife. You stand with your back toward me. I'm taller than you, and I'm going to knife you."

"I thought it was only wedlock you wanted."

"Later."

He jabbed the stick on her back.

"Well? Get anything?"

"Nothing," said Bill softly, "but a chance to put my arms around you and say—"

"You'll only be marrying a widow." Sue turned and looked at him.

"With such a soft light in your eyes, what do you mean, a widow?"

"I'm worried."

"Look at all the life insurance you'll get." He held her close to him.

"How much, darling?"

"They pay double for accidents. You'll get two grand, only—"

"Only what, dear?" Sue asked, playing with his hair.

"Only . . . I've borrowed . . . quite a lot on it."

"That's all right. I'm a generous little soul. . . . Mr. Benedict, I've decided to take your proposal seriously. There's nothing like being a virgin, a wife, and a widow all in a week."

"Tally-ho," cried Bill and kissed her.

"I'm no fox, my sweet."

"We'll get married by a magistrate and have a wedding break-fast at the Lafayette. For our honeymoon—"

"We'll take a nice streamlined subway to Kew Gardens and find a refrigerator and a porch. What else do you need in a house?"

"A bed!" He reached for a bottle of beer.

"No more murders."

"Damn, where's that bottle opener?" Bill was trying to hold the bottle in one hand and Sue in the other.

"On the floor."

Bill dropped Sue and the bottle on the bed. Sue picked up the champagne swizzle stick. "I've got to get that insurance money one way or another." Playfully, she stabbed the stick into Bill's back. He let out a howl, and suddenly stopped.

"Hit me again," he cried. He remained bending.

"I'm marrying a masochist." She jabbed him again.

"Oh, my sweet Sue," Bill yelped, getting up quickly. "You know where you hit me?"

"Sure, on your back."

"But what part?" He tore off his shirt to show his bare back.

"Why, a torso!"

"Torso, hell. You've knocked the Murray case wide open again."

"I thought it was you I hit."

"That's just it."

The phone rang. It was Potts to inform Bill that he didn't have to hide out any more.

"Until you got Mr. X behind bars, I'll stay right here."

Potts chuckled. "I know who Mr. X is."

"What! Who is he?"

"I ain't tellin'."

"Do I know him?" Bill yelled.

"You know him."

"Jesus, Potts, I get bruised all over trying to help you solve a crime, and what do I get in return?"

"And what about me?" Sue shouted into the phone. "Do I get first whack for the *Examiner?*"

Potts sighed. "You'll both get what you want."

"Can you tell us how you found out?"

"Nope."

"Can you say when you're going to make the arrest?"

"Nope."

"Is it someone we've never heard of?"

"Nope."

"Are you still quite sane, Mr. Potts?"

"Nope— What?" He hung up.

Bill paced the floor, his mouth set in a suspicious scowl. He kept fondling the swizzle stick. "And just a while back, I thought I had such a good clue."

Sue sat a long while without talking; then she walked over and put a hand in Bill's. "I want to be serious for a minute."

"Go ahead."

"I want you to stop making believe you're Sherlock Holmes."

"Darling, I never claimed to be anything but a press agent."

"Will you keep on being one, and stop trying to out-Philo Vance."

"Listen, my sweet, I don't go around yelling, 'Trouble, come to papa!'"

"Why did you mess around with Laney?"

"Because when Charlie Beach was killed, I've got a good right to feel that I may be next."

Sue considered for a moment. "Let's get out of town."

"Not until Mr. X has row AA in Sing Sing."

She looked up at Bill sharply. "Did you tell Potts that Nick Finley admitted that he was in your room the night Leo was killed? Or that he's tied up with Laney?"

Bill stared off into space.

"Did you?"

"No."

"Why not?"

"Because according to Potts' own reports Nick has perfect alibis for everything."

"But why did he want to get rid of you?"

Bill pondered a moment. "Something mighty big is frightening Nick. And I'll be goddamned if I know what it is." Bill reached over to the night table for a box of medicine. He put a capsule in his mouth.

"Hey," Sue warned. "That's the third one and that's too many. You ought to let sleeping pills lie."

"Not . . . the way I feel," Bill said and turned over.

The next morning, Nick's secretary informed Bill that Nick had left town and she didn't know where he'd gone.

"If he calls up in a hurry and wants me," Bill said, "I'll be over at Leo Murray's office."

"The late Leo Murray?" the girl said sarcastically.

Bill nodded irritably.

Bill's walk from Finley's office to Murray's covered approximately three and a half city blocks. It was eleven o'clock in the morning and the first theatrical birds were already out looking for worms. Bill knew most of them and it took him nearly an hour to get through. Everybody had a question about the Charlie Beach murder. Bill was greeted and buttonholed, like an "angel" with enough money to back a season of shows.

At 46th Street a gang of permanent curb kibitzers cornered Bill. He had to be a good fellow and answer all questions. If he didn't, Broadway would say he was suffering from a bad case of front-pageitis. Main Street was quick to resent any reticence on the part of one of its villagers. If the breaks were bad, Broadway wanted to help; if they were good, Broadway wanted to be helped. Either way, the habitués of Wisecrack Canyon hungered passionately to be in on the know.

At the Regent Theater Building Angus, the elevator man, had to have his say.

"Charlie Beach shuah musta knowed too much."

"Yeah," Bill said, weary of the whole thing.

"I suppose if you did see the killer, you ain't tellin'."

"I didn't see him," Bill said quickly.

"I expect you wouldn't say if yo' had."

"Take me up, will you, Angus. And let's forget the whole thing."

"Hell," said Angus a little indignantly. "Yore right in the center of things. But I ain't. I'm curious."

"I'm not."

A man stepped into the lobby and walked to the elevator.

"Goin' up?" Angus sang.

The man got in. He was short, like a stub-pencil. "Harmon and Hart?"

"Third floor."

The elevator creaked its way up. Bill got out at the second. As the elevator passed him, he looked intently through the grill at the short man. The elevator clanged to a stop on the third floor. Bill waited to hear the man's steps on the marble above him. Then he heard a door close.

Bill rang the elevator bell. Angus returned to the second floor.

"Angus, you know everybody in town. Did you ever see that man before?"

Angus shook his head.

"You sure?"

"Yeah."

"I thought he might be some out of town critic."

"Maybe," said Angus, and started the elevator downward.

The Murray office was empty. But from the end of the hall came the sound of a typewriter. Bill walked toward it and opened the door to Murray's private office.

Ricky Linton was sitting at Leo's desk typing. He looked up quickly. A flush filled his face.

"You know you're fired, don't you?" he said slowly.

"I heard rumors."

"You heard right."

"Where there's smoke, there's firing, eh?"

"That stinks. Get out."

Bill shrugged and turned to go.

"Wait a minute. I want to talk to you. Sit down."

He pointed to a chair.

"I'm a busy man, Linton."

"This is important."

"Okay."

Linton started typing again.

"I'm still a busy man."

"When I'm through, you'll see why it's worth waiting for."

Bill walked around the room and studied the photographs on the wall. Leo Murray with Ina Claire, Leo with Fay Bainter and Jane Cowl; Leo with Alice Lawrence; Leo with Daniel Frohman and Irving Berlin; Leo with Maxwell Anderson; and Leo.

Linton finished typing. He pulled the page from the machine, folded it and put it in his pocket. "Benedict, how long did Boley work for Leo?"

"As long as Leo's been in the business."

"How long is that?"

"Close to fifteen years." Bill moved closer to the door as Linton got out of his chair and walked up and down the office.

"Leo trust Boley?"

"Sure."

Bill watched him stop and light a cigarette. The fingers were unsteady.

"I think," he said finally, in a suddenly high-pitched voice, "I know who murdered Leo."

"So do the cops," said Bill indifferently.

"Why don't they make an arrest then?"

"Listen, Linton, I'm just an errand boy around here. I take care of publicity and the cops take care of crime. We got an arrangement. They don't butt into my business. I don't butt into theirs."

Linton's lips twisted in a bitter curve. "They're making it my business. I got tickets to sail on the *Normandie* next week. Me and Alice. They say I can't."

"Too bad. The dear little honeymooners can't go to the dear Riviera when they want to. Tsk. Tsk."

"They got a vault for those wisecracks in Kentucky."

"Okay, Linton. Is that all you wanted to tell me?"

"I wanted to tell you that Frank Boley has been robbing Leo Murray for years."

"What are Yale's chances for the Rose Bowl?"

"I've been going over the books and figures. For this show alone, the production cost according to Boley's figures is seventy-five grand. Scenery and lighting come to $22,000. I checked up with the builders and Eddie Cook of Century Lighting. They say that all they charged between them is $12,100. Where did the other $10,000 come from? From Mr. Boley's generous fountain pen. And where did it go? To Mr. Boley's pocket."

Bill sat down. "I hear from the G.O.P.," he said casually, "that James Farley steals two-cent stamps from post offices."

"All right, don't believe me. Look at the books. He's charged us—I had fifty per cent of the show—for five more stage-hands than we have. His prop account alone has a discrepancy of over a thousand dollars. And if he did it with this show, can you imagine how he's been rooking Leo right along?"

"Have you talked to Boley?"

"He hasn't shown up here since the funeral. I tried to reach him and I can't."

"What makes you think he killed Leo . . . and Charlie?"

"Motive, you damned fool! Leo found out that Boley was gypping him. Leo threatened to tell all. Boley kills him to protect himself, then kills Charlie because maybe Charlie knows too much. It fits like a rubber girdle."

"Like a pair of oversized slacks, you mean. What about Boley's alibi the night of the murder?"

"So what? He says he was in the box office from seven o'clock on. Who vouches for that? The regular box-office man. But who vouches for him? Nobody. Don't you think maybe he kept his mouth shut for a couple of grand?" Linton kicked a wastepaper basket over. "What's a couple of grand to a four star thief like Boley?"

"Going to tell the cops?" Bill settled back in his chair.

"First of all I want the money back, if there's any left. Then you can tell the cops."

"How are you going to get it back?"

"I'll threaten Boley with exposure unless he hands it over."

"And if he does you'll expose him anyway, eh?"

"Sure," said Linton lightly.

"Just a loyal member of society. It happens I like Boley. I don't believe he would have murdered Leo even if it meant twenty years for embezzlement. He loved that guy. He was the only one on

Broadway who did." He took a long breath, lit a cigarette and looked over the flame into Linton's eyes. "You're not going to double-cross him."

"I'll get you wangled in on this as an accessory after the fact," Linton said, smiling mirthlessly.

"What fact?"

Linton pulled the phone across the desk toward him. He started to dial. Bill put his finger down on the bar.

"What's the idea?" Linton demanded.

"Give me a couple of hours, Ricky. I'll try to find Boley and get the money back for you. If I don't you can call the cops. If I do, maybe I'll know whether Boley killed Leo." He paused and stabbed his cigarette onto an ash tray. "I'm doing this—getting the money back—only because half of it goes to Ruth."

Linton dropped the receiver on the hooks. "Okay."

"I trust you," said Bill, "like the Pope trusts Mussolini." His eyes became cold and level. "So if you double-cross me and call the cops the moment I'm out of here, I'm going to get a warrant out for Alice Lawrence on a charge of moral turpitude, and make such a fuss she won't be able to get a visa for Great Britain."

Ricky Linton's face tightened and he swung a heavy hand at Bill. Bill expected it and side-stepped neatly. With the top of his head he butted Linton under the jaw. Linton fell across the desk like a sack of books.

"Can't say it wasn't in self-defense," Bill murmured to the unconscious figure. He cut the phone wire and dragged Linton to the toilet, locked the door and put the key in his pocket.

Bill walked to the outer office. The stubby man he had seen in the elevator was sitting quietly on a chair.

"What do you want?"

The little man looked up at him with a dozy expression on his face.

"Please, when I can see the producer?" the man asked mildly.

"What for?"

The man pulled a brief-case from under his coat. "I'd like him to read a play I wrote."

"He's gone out of business. No play today. Called on account of murder. Beat it."

The man rose apologetically. "I thought someone had taken over Mr. Murray's business."

"Not yet. The office is closed until further notice."

"Thank you." And he walked to the elevator with Bill.

When they got out on the street, Bill took a cab. The stubby man also took a cab.

CHAPTER XVI
TWO SCOTCHES GO TO HELL

Bill spent the rest of the day in a frantic search for Frank Boley. He tried all the conventional cubicles of drink from the Café Deauville to Dinty Moore's, from Jack and Charlie's to John the Swede's on West 10th Street. No one had seen Boley.

At six o'clock, he called Ruth Murray.

"Ruth? This is Bill Benedict."

"I'm glad you called, Bill."

"Do you know where I can reach Frank Boley?"

"No. Anything wrong?"

"No."

"Bill, I'd like to see you."

"Sure. When?"

Her voice broke. "As soon as you can make it."

"I'll be right over."

Then he telephoned Sue and made a date to meet her at Ruth's.

Ruth met him at the door. She was dressed in a dark purple lounging gown of some kind of shiny and stiff material. Her hair had recently been washed and fixed and was combed high on her head. Her lips were reddened by lipstick, and there was a hectic light in her eyes.

They sat down.

"I'll get you a drink in a moment, Bill." Her voice was high-pitched and tense, "but first I must ask you— It's—terrible about Charlie."

Bill nodded.

"Do you—or the police think there's any connection between Leo's death—and Charlie's?"

"Yes." Bill avoided her eyes.

"When will it stop?" she whispered.

"When they catch the murderer."

"I hope to God it's today. The papers say that the police know who it is. Is that so?"

"So the papers say. Lieutenant Potts told me he knew."

Ruth's eyes widened with tears. "Did he tell you who?"

"No."

She rose and walked to the window, pressing her hands. "I've prayed, Bill. I really have—for the first time since I was a girl. I've prayed that the murderer will be caught soon. He must be. Not so much that I want to avenge Leo. But because I'm afraid. . . . I'm afraid—others might die. Like Charlie. . . ." She sat down in a corner chair and dropped her head in her hands. "I'm horribly frightened."

Bill walked over to her. "Ruth . . . Why don't you go out of town for a week or so? It'll be all over by then."

"It's so terrible, Bill. One thing leads to another. . . . One murder brings a second . . . and maybe a third." She placed frightened fingers over her mouth. "Who will be—the next?"

"Why haven't you called me before?"

"I haven't called anyone."

"But you're taking this alone."

She hesitated. "I didn't know who to trust." Then smiling wanly: "I don't mean you."

"The cops know the murderer; they've got their eye on him—"

"Then why haven't they arrested him?"

"It'll come."

Ruth got up, brushed her hair back and walked toward the kitchen. "I'll make us a couple of highballs."

"They'll help. But before you do, let's get something over with—something unpleasant, and then we can drink on an easy mind and an empty stomach."

"Yes?" The word came in a quick intake of breath. She stood at the door expectantly.

"Was Leo ever married—secretly?"

Her face paled and two round spots of rouge stood out on her cheeks.

"Or did he have any children that the world didn't know of?"

Ruth lifted her head high and looked steadily at Bill. "No. What made you ask?"

"I just had a hunch, that's all. I thought you'd know." Bill picked a cigarette out of a box and tapped it.

"No. Of course, I don't know everything about Leo's private life." She wet her lips. "Why did you ask me on the phone about Frank?"

"Do you know where he is?"

"At his hotel or the office. Why?"

"Linton says he has the evidence to show that Frank's been gypping Leo out of a lot of money."

"Oh, my God! No! That's a lie! It's impossible! Frank wouldn't do such a thing. Leo trusted him." She walked hurriedly to the telephone. "I'll get hold of him and prove I'm right."

"Don't bother. He's not at his hotel. He's not at the office. He's not anywhere."

She sat down suddenly and stared at Bill.

"Are you keeping anything from me? Has Frank been arrested? Has he?"

"No."

"I don't believe you. That man's innocent. They'll kill him. He mustn't be arrested." She was talking wildly.

"That's why I've got to find him before the night's over. And, one way or the other, I'm going to get him to talk."

"Yes," Ruth said, rising from the seat and going toward the kitchen door again. "Yes, find Frank and talk to him. Of course, that's the thing to do." Color returned to her cheeks. "I'll make those drinks, now." She went into the kitchen.

Bill looked at his watch. It was close to six o'clock. He looked around the living room. There were few signs of Leo's personality. A couple of modern photographs on the wall and two water colors, one by John Marin and the other by L.P.S. completed the decor. There were books on the theater, on psychoanalysis and history.

Bill pulled from its place Lawson's *Technique of Playwriting*. He found Leo's name in the index and looked at the reference to see if he had marked it. The page was clean. He closed the book and was about to replace it when he noticed some pamphlets in the empty space behind. Curious, he took them out. He looked at them closely and made a note of the titles on the inside of a match packet. Hearing Ruth coming he put them back.

"Leo had a fine library," he said.

Ruth was a few feet behind him with two highballs on a tray.

"Yes."

The doorbell rang.

"Answer it, Bill."

It was Sue dressed in a new coat and snap-down gray hat.

"As fresh as a Kamchatka salmon," greeted Bill. He stuck his cheek forward. "A kiss!"

Ruth said hello in a thin voice. "We're just having a drink. Join us?"

"As soon as I get rid of this parasite." She kissed Bill.

"You see," Bill crowed. "I'm under her skin already."

Ruth turned to go back into the kitchen. Her knee hit the telephone table. The tray slid out of her hands and crashed to the floor.

"Oh, hell!" Bill said. "There goes two perfectly good Scotches." He plucked out a handkerchief. "I'll sop it up for you, Ruth."

"Thanks, don't bother. It's nothing. I'll get a mop."

"No! I got to impress Sue with my housewifely manners." He got on his knees and wiped up the liquid. "Bill, the old Dartmouth biddy."

"Don't bother, please," Ruth said, embarrassed. She had a mop and pushed Bill away. "Now, give me your handkerchief. I'll have it laundered."

"I wouldn't think of it."

"But you got it dirty on my floor."

Bill lifted her into the kitchen. "Go on, make those drinks and stop chaffering."

Ruth hesitated. "I'm all out of Scotch."

"Good," said Sue. "Let's go out and eat." She put her arm around Bill and Ruth. "What do you say?"

Ruth shook her head. "You go ahead without me. I don't like going out these days."

"It'll be a pick-me-up," said Sue.

"I'd rather not, please." Ruth passed a hand over her face and trembled slightly. "I'm terribly tired. I think I'll go to bed early tonight. Thanks anyway."

"We can bring the food up here."

"No. Many thanks, but I'd rather be alone."

"Where to now, Benedict?" Sue asked, when they got to the street.

"We've got to go and see a man."

"About a dog?"

"No—about a murder."

CHAPTER XVII
THE CASE OF THE UNLUCKY BENEDICT

At a Childs where they had dinner, Bill made a half dozen telephone calls.

He explained to Sue. "We've got to find Frank Boley tonight if he's anywhere in the city. I've called some good friends. They're going to help."

"How."

"I called Jim Correll. He's a longshoreman. Within an hour all the bars and saloons from the Battery to 59th Street will be covered on the West Side. I described Boley to him, and he'll keep an eye out for him. Then, I called Chet Rabinowitz. He'll make a quick survey of the gin centers of Fulton Street, Brooklyn. Vincent Gomez will do the same for Harlem, and I've got Serlin covering Greenwich Village, the East Side, the hotels, and the night spots."

"My God! A veritable octopus."

"Eat! In an hour we leave here to cover the city like an American Legion convention."

The hour went by and the reports coming in were discouraging. Boley was either out of the city or had suddenly joined the Woman's Christian Temperance Union.

Bill had all calls transferred to his hotel room where he and Sue played Truth and Consequences until three o'clock. Then the call finally came through. It was from Harlem. Boley was seen at Mattie's near the old Cotton Club.

Bill and Sue splurged on a taxi.

"What are you going to say to Boley when you see him?" Sue asked.

"The spirit of the night'll move me."

"Just one of the Mardi Gras boys."

"It would be nice," Bill said, wearily tossing his cigarette at the flanks of a passing Lincoln, "to enter Mr. Potts' office dramatically and beat him to it by carrying the culprit along by the scruff of his neck."

"Frank Boley doesn't have a scruff."

Bill laid his head on Sue's bosom and closed his eyes. "Let me think, will you?"

"Who am I to resist a struggling impulse? Now I'll know what a detective looks like when he raticionates."

Bill was quiet.

"You heard me. You look pretty raticionating."

"The word's rat—raticinating."

"Raticionating!"

"Raticinating."

"What does it mean, anyway?"

Bill disengaged himself and lit a cigarette. "It's what I was trying to do before you so ruthlessly interrupted."

"What was that?"

"It's what detectives do. Aristotle started it. The Scholastics added their widow's mite, and today anybody who takes Philosophy 1 knows that ratication is a process of deduction and conclusion and premise and a priori and syllogism and perilepsis and empirema. In short the horns of a dilemma that are brought together. Now, do you see?"

"I don't care what it is, it's still raticionation," Sue said winningly.

"It's raticination."

"It's a Hundred and Thirty-Fifth Street, mister," the driver said.

Mattie's was a little-known semi-public drinking place off Seventh Avenue. They went through a garden alley cut between two tenements, then up to a wooden door with the name painted on it.

A huge Mulatto woman, Mattie, greeted Bill and waved an arm to a table. Boley was sitting at it, head in hands, asleep.

"He's been here since close to midnight. Passed out once or twice but we brung him to."

"Thanks, Mattie." They sat down at Boley's table. Mattie brought them drinks.

They drank in silence. The door opened and a couple of girls came in. Then a white man. Bill held his eyes on Boley. The man was beginning to move slowly. Bill nudged Sue, and both of them watched.

Boley grunted once or twice, then slowly picked up his head. He had a two-day beard, his pale eyes were shot with blood, and around the corners of his lips was a hard, brown crust of saliva. He fumbled over his glass of stale beer like a blind man. Then he saw Bill. The glass rolled out of his fingers. He leaned back in his chair, his hand automatically reaching to straighten his tie. He grinned. "H'lo."

"Hello, Frank. You know Sue, don't you?"

Frank nodded heavily. "I been expectin' you—or someone."

"Where have you been, Frank?"

"Round. Don' know. Who wansa—know? Cops?"

"Why did you disappear?"

"Who?"

"No one could find you."

"Diden know where—to look." He reached over and patted Bill's hand. "You—found me. Diden ya?"

"Come on home with us, Frank."

Boley shook his head deliberately. "No."

"Can you understand what I'm saying?"

"Sure."

"Ricky Linton has found out that the accounts on *Hour's End* are cockeyed."

"Sure."

"You know about it?"

"Sure."

"You took the money then?"

Boley tried to focus his eyes on Bill. He shook his head to clear it of the fog. "What ya say?"

"You gypped Leo Murray out of ten grand."

Boley sighed. His facial muscles flexed. He reflected on something, then he sighed again and grinned like a small boy caught with the jam.

"Yea . . . Sure . . . More than ten gran'."

"Why?"

"Lea' me alone, will ya."

"Why did you kill Leo?"

Boley rose in his chair and bellowed: "Get outta here! Bastard! Get out!"

Mattie came over. "You'll have to shut him up." Bill pulled Boley back to his chair.

"Okay," he said. "You didn't kill Leo. But why did you rob the pants off him?"

Boley waved the question away and said, "Ask Leo."

Bill scribbled a note and gave it to Boley. "Frank, listen carefully. Linton's going to charge you with embezzlement tomorrow morning—probably'll insinuate murder. You'll have a lot of explaining to do and you'll need a good lawyer. I've written down the name and address of a friend of mine. He'll do what he can for you. Do you want to go to his home now or in the morning?"

Boley closed his eyes. "Don' need—lawyer."

Bill called Mattie over and paid for the drinks.

"There may be a little fuss here for a moment or so. I'm going to take him out with us."

"Okay. Only don't break no chairs or anything."

Bill grinned. "I'll pay for what's broken." He turned to Sue. "Go outside and get a taxi ready."

"There's someone over there looking at you, Bill."

Bill glanced at a table in a niche to one side. The short, stubby man was sitting there.

"Hey you." Bill walked over to him.

"Speaking to me?" the man said evenly.

"What are you following me for?"

"I never saw you before."

"You're the guy who wants a play produced."

"Go away, buddy, you're tight."

"If I see you again tonight or tomorrow, my size or no my size, I'm going to bust you wide open."

The little man grinned sourly. "It's up to you, buddy."

Mattie came over to Bill. "There's a cab waiting."

Boley let himself be taken to the taxi without protest.

Bill helped Boley undress. Halfway through, Boley got sick and went into the bathroom. Bill rang downstairs.

"Send up some more towels, will you?" He hung up. "Everything okay, Frank?"

Bill heard a groan and the noise of a body falling. He ran into the bathroom. Boley was on the floor, blood streaming from his throat. Bill tried to pick him up but the man was too heavy. Then he tied a towel around Boley's neck and ran back to the telephone. "Send a doctor right up!"

When Bill got back to the bathroom, Boley was dying. His washed-out eyes were fastened on Bill's, and there was a curious grin on his face. Bill looked away. Then he saw something scrawled in soap on the bathroom mirror.

TELL POLICE I KILLED MURRAY
BOLEY

When the house doctor arrived, Bill telephoned Potts.

"Don't let anybody wipe that soap off the mirror," the detective shouted after Bill had completed telling him the events of the day. "I'll be right over."

Bill communicated Potts' orders to the doctor. "And when Mr. Potts comes tell him he can find me in Miss Huxley's room."

As Bill entered Sue's room, the short, stub-pencil man was just closing a door of a room across the hall.

Sue was still dressed. He flopped down on her bed.

"Boley's dead. Committed suicide. He's in my room now. He confessed everything. I've already called Potts. Have you got ten fingers of Scotch?"

Sue poured out a drink for Bill; then one for herself.

"For God's sakes, Sue, don't look so damned shocked."

"An awful lot of gore has flowed under the bridge," she said slowly.

"And me in every drop of it. Benedict, the mortician's best friend. No murder is legal without me!" He struck a match savagely.

"Take it easy, boy."

Bill crossed the room to a window and picked up the shade. It was getting light. Below on Broadway, milk and ice wagons were making deliveries.

"So, Frank Boley did it," he mused. "A generous, Tammany ward-heeling dipsomaniac whom you'd have thought had never cherished an idea more criminal than double-crossing a ticket-broker. Frank Boley murdered two men." He turned on Sue. "Damn it, it's hard to believe. Why did he kill? To hide the fact that he embezzled? Christ, all he'd have to do was to explain to Ruth. She wouldn't have pressed charges against him. She'd have let him pay it back to her." He became silent and gulped down the rest of his Scotch. "Ruth's going to take this the hard way. She swore that Frank didn't steal the money. Now she'll find out he killed her brother."

The door opened and Potts stood before them, a grin of triumph immobilizing his lips, his legs spread apart like a blue-serged Colossus of Rhodes. "Well?"

"I beat you to it, Potts. I found your murderer for you," Bill said.

"So you told me on the telephone."

"Surprised?"

Potts considered for a moment. Then he rapped his hands together in disgust.

"Boley confesses. 'Tell the police I killed Murray.' How did he get in and out of your room without no one seeing him? How did he arrange to shoot Beach? Or did he?"

"Try a spiritualist. Maybe Boley'll answer from wherever he is," Bill said. "You told us the other day you knew who the murderer was. Were you right or wrong? Now, honestly."

Potts looked at Bill strangely.

"Right or wrong, Potts?"

"Fifty-fifty."

"Now, that's a damned confusing thing to say. Were you right or were you wrong?"

Potts shrugged and sighed. "I got work to do."

"Walking out on us?"

"It'll save," Potts said.

"Will you do me a favor, Potts?"

"What?" Potts looked at him suspiciously.

"Keep Boley's confession out of the papers."

Potts' round face lit up like a headlight. "Gladly," he said and left the room.

CHAPTER XVIII
PROLOGUE TO THE THIRD ACT

When Bill put on his shoes the next morning, he saw that they had bloodstains from the night before. He reached into his laundry bag for a soiled handkerchief. Linen was as good as anything else to wipe shoes with. Something on the handkerchief stopped him. He let the bloodstains remain and took the handkerchief over to the window. He fingered the linen carefully, then pulled at a corner. It tore off easily. Bill whistled softly and wet his lips that had suddenly gone dry. He got an envelope from a drawer and placed the handkerchief inside.

The day was an active one for Bill. He sent a telegram to Albany and signed it William Benedict, Deputy Sheriff. He made a call at a chemical laboratory and during the late afternoon took a trip via the Hudson Tubes to Jersey City. He looked up an address on a residential street and hung around the corner until ten o'clock. He got home by midnight, found an answer from Albany and with a very unhappy expression on his face, slept the restless sleep of the damned.

He was awakened at seven by Potts on the phone.

"Can't you let a guy sleep?" Bill said.

"What've been doing?"

"Sleeping."

"No, yesterday."

"Nothing."

"Liar."

"Sticks and stones. . . ."

"Do ya expect to live in Jersey City after you're married?"

"Not if they sliced it up and garnished it with mother of pearl."

"Then what were ya doing over there yesterday?"

Bill was silent for a moment; then hung up. It would take Potts at least ten minutes to get over to the Chicopee. He'd have to dress quickly. In five minutes by Bill's Ingersoll, he was out of the room. Instead of taking the elevator, he walked down the stairs. Halfway in the first flight, he heard footsteps behind him. It was the stubby man he had seen up at Mattie's. Bill waited until the man came abreast of him.

"Little man, I told you that the next time I saw you would be too many times. Now, who the hell are you?"

The man grinned. "Just coincidence, buddy."

"Okay, Mister." Bill made a gesture to him to go ahead. The man looked chagrined and walked downstairs. Bill hurried back to his room. He waited a couple of minutes and then leaned out of the window. The man was standing on the sidewalk in front of the hotel entrance.

"You can't watch two places at the same time," Bill said aloud. He took the elevator to the basement, and went out the delivery entrance.

Ten minutes too late Potts drove up to the Chicopee in a police car. He saw the sawed-off little man walking up and down.

"What the hell are you doing here, Nelson?" Nelson pointed upstairs.

"He's beat it."

"Why ain't you with him?"

"He caught up with me. Took the elevator to the basement and got out that way. I can't be back there and up here at the same time."

"Come on. We got to hurry down to the D.A.'s office."

Henry Traube was in when they arrived. He made them sit down and passed out post-election cigars. "I've been waiting for this, Potts."

"Mr. Traube," Potts said directly, "four days ago Leo Murray was stabbed to death in Bill Benedict's room. Your office left the case entirely in my hands. Ya ain't pressed me and ya ain't raised a stink, and I'm grateful. It's the hardest case I ever had charge of. Nothing to go on. I been playing the cards my own way. Now, I feel I got to lay 'em on the table for ya."

"One minute, Lieutenant. If you don't mind, I want a girl to take down everything you say. I'd like to keep a record of your report."

Potts nodded, and the D.A. rang for a stenographer.

"Go ahead, Mr. Potts."

"At first I figured that Charlie Beach was a very hot prospect. He disappeared, and in my experience that's as good a clue as any. Then he sends Bill Benedict—the feller ya gave an alibi for—a note to meet him. Benedict goes to pick him up and Beach is knocked off. Mind ya—that was the second murder with Benedict somewhere around."

Traube looked concerned. "Are you suspecting Benedict?"

Potts waved a heavy hand. "Let me continue this story."

"Okay."

"That phony telegram signed by John Wilkes Booth which was sent to the sister of the deceased was found by Benedict. Benedict again!"

"He reported it to you, didn't he?"

"Sure. I figured at that time everything was legitimate. Then one day I'm with Benedict and his girl when a message comes to him warning him to lay off putting his nose in the case any further. What can ya deduct from that message, I asked myself. *The murderer thinks we know more than we actually do!* And the truth is, I didn't have a shadder of an idea about the identity of the murderer—then! Now, if the murderer thinks we know more than we do, says I, why not goose him along and play in with him? So I gave a statement to the papers—with your permission, you remember—that a quick arrest was on the cards. In this way, the murderer might lose his head and make an open break."

"But the warning message was sent to Benedict?"

"Sure. That's the point. I decide that maybe the murderer will make an attempt on Benedict's life. So I assign Nelson here—" he pointed to the squat man who was sitting in the corner paring his nails—"to tail him. Which he does." Potts relaxed and breathed a long sigh. "No attempt is made on Benedict's life. That's number one. Second, he finds Boley—and all of a sudden, out of a clear sky, Boley commits suicide and confesses. Where? *In Benedict's room!* Third, according to Nelson, Benedict's been acting damned mysterious. He goes to a chemical lab, he fools around all day in Jersey, and when I speak to him this morning he hangs up on me and double tracks Nelson, and maybe, at this very minute, is trying to beat it out of town."

"You concluded, therefore, that he sent himself the warning message?"

"Yep!"

"That he killed Murray? And Beach to protect himself for some reason; then Boley to mislead the police? Is that right?"

Potts hesitated a fraction of a second. "I been wrong before, Mr. Traube. On Charlie Beach, for example. Then there was Laney. I got a search call out for him. *And* it was *Benedict* who put me on Laney, without telling me a thing. Every time I take a step in this case, I find that Benedict guy. Maybe with only one exception. Nick Finley. He didn't have much of an alibi. And as far as I can remember Benedict never mentioned that guy to me but once—and that was to say Finley offered him a job. From that time on, Finley's out of the picture. Personally, I think there's a tie-up between them. It's damned funny that Benedict works for the one suspect who's dropped out. So you see, Mr. Traube, I got to take action."

"It's impossible." The D.A. got up from his desk and stared at Potts.

"That's the very point, Mr. D.A. You gave Benedict his alibi. You was having dinner with him at the time of the murder. Are ya sure?"

"Of course!"

Potts rubbed his hands together desperately. "Did he leave ya for five minutes? What time did ya meet him?"

"You've sure put me on a spot, Lieutenant." Traube passed his hand over his eyes. "I know we had dinner together approximately between seven and eight."

"You didn't see him before seven?"

"No."

"Then it *is* possible, Mr. Traube. Maybe the Medical Examiner was wrong by an hour. That happens. He can only tell generally speaking when a murder's been committed."

"What do you want me to do?"

"I want a warrant from your office for the arrest of William Benedict on the charge of murdering Murray, Beach, and Boley."

"On purely circumstantial evidence?"

"Yes. I'm sure if he answers certain questions that he'll have to answer, we'll have a sight more than circumstantial evidence."

"I'll not be able to prosecute. Someone else'll have to do it."

"I understand, Mr. Traube."

The district attorney walked to the window silently and looked out on the street. "All right, Potts. You get the warrant."

Bill called Sue from a pay station. She was still in her room at the Chicopee.

"Sue, listen. If Potts calls you don't tell him you spoke to me."

"What's the matter?"

"He wants to see me, and the feeling's not mutual. How is it your paper hasn't run the Boley suicide story?"

"I phoned it in, but the Police Department and the D.A.'s office ordered it to be held up. None of the papers'll have it. . . . You're not going places and get beat up again, are you?"

"Are you dressed, honey?"

"Thirty-three and a third per cent."

"Put on the other two-thirds, go down to Potts' precinct house and see what you can find out. There's no hurry, but if you think there's something I ought to know call me at Ruth Murray's. But call from a pay station. With love and kisses, sincerely yours."

Bill hopped a bus to Ruth's house. He waited until the elevator had gone up to answer a call, then took the stairs. He rang the apartment bell. There was no answer. He waited and rang again. Ruth opened the door. She looked surprised. Her hair was upset, and she was wearing a house-dress. There were crates on the floor.

"Bill, is there something wrong?"

He followed her into the living room. The door leading into the bedroom was closed.

"Are you moving, Ruth?"

She sat down on the couch helplessly. "I can't continue to live in this place. Too many memories."

"Sue and I are getting married."

"Oh, Bill!" She went over to him and took his hand warmly. "I'm so glad for your sake." She remained standing. "It was sweet of you to come over and tell me."

"I saw Frank Boley last night."

Ruth pushed back her hair nervously. "He told you Linton was a liar, didn't he?"

"No."

"I don't believe it!"

"It's true. Frank *did* steal money from Leo on the production and running cost. Thousands of dollars."

She walked to the door. "If that's your news there's no point to it. I don't believe you. . . . I'm busy. I've got a lot to do."

"Why did Frank have to steal?"

She leaned forward, intense and angry. "Not until he tells me himself, will I believe it."

"Frank's dead."

She stood at the door transfixed, the color rushed out of her face, and she began to pant as if she were about to sob aloud. Then, slowly, she walked to a chair and sat down.

"Frank dead!"

"He killed himself."

She began to weep softly.

"He died in my room."

"Did he . . . have anything to say?"

"Yes. . . ."

She lifted her eyes and kept them steadily on Bill. Suddenly she paled and looked past Bill to the bedroom door. A long sigh came from her lips. "One minute, please." She spoke slowly and with dignity, and walked to the bedroom door. She opened it. "Lee . . ." she called softly.

A little boy about ten years old, his dark eyes and proud face full of questions, entered the room. "Lee, this is an old friend of your father's. . . ." She turned to Bill. "This is my nephew. Leo Murray's son."

The boy shook hands gravely; then looked at Ruth inquiringly.

"Lee, do me a favor, please, and walk in the Park for a while. I'd like to talk with Bill alone." He nodded. "The doorman will see that you cross the street all right."

"Good-by, Mr. Benedict. Please come again." He turned to Ruth. "I'll be at the reservoir, if you want me, Aunt Ruth."

He left the room.

Bill followed the boy out with his eyes. Ruth walked over to a window facing the reservoir. She watched silently until she saw the doorman leading Lee across the street. Bill crossed to the window and watched with her. Then, the two of them turned and faced each other. Ruth's eyes were filled with tears. Bill puffed away at his cold pipe angrily.

The door buzzer rang. Ruth shot an anxious look at Bill. He shrugged and opened the door. There was quite a little crowd standing on the other side of the threshold: Lieutenant Potts, Nick Finley, Laney—and the little man.

Bill tried to hide his surprise. "Come in, boys," he said. "Everybody knows everybody else? Ah, with one exception. Ruth, this is Jock Laney, alias Lawrence, alias Lewis, etc."

Laney's face darkened.

Potts muttered an apology to Ruth and they all sat down.

"Would you mind telling me how you knew I was here, Potts?" Bill asked.

"Ya ain't so smart, Benedict," Potts said antagonistically. "Ya forgot that everybody connected with this case has been tailed. Well—" He nodded toward Ruth. "The guy assigned to Miss Murray here called me to say ya had arrived. That's clear, ain't it?"

"I guess I ain't so smart," Bill said thoughtfully.

"You're a dope on wheels," Laney said. Finley smiled evenly and kept his silence.

"Bill," Potts said a trifle uneasily, "Laney says he saw you at the Hotel Chicopee a little after seven the night Murray was murdered."

Bill smiled suddenly. "Me? So it's me you've brought this cavalcade along for?"

"Who else?" snarled Laney.

Bill shook his head. "Laney says I was at the Chicopee at seven. Besides being a liar his jail record ought to prove even to you, Potts, he's a blackmailing crook."

Laney took a step toward Bill. The little man stepped between them.

"Nelson," Potts instructed the little man, "keep Laney in his place." Nelson took a gun out of his holster and put it in his pocket.

"Potts, you're cockeyed as hell on this," Bill said.

The huge man chewed noisily. "Nick Finley corroborates Laney."

"What?" Bill turned to Finley. "You saw me too?"

Finley sighed uncomfortably. "Yeah."

Bill laughed. "Nice work, boys." He pointed his pipe at Potts. "What about Henry Traube's statement that he was having dinner with me at the time Leo was murdered?"

"He says he ain't willing to swear that ya was with him at seven. It might've been seven-fifteen or seven-thirty. That's within the possible time of Murray's death."

"So— You've got me placed at the scene of the crime—at the time of the crime."

"All this is direct evidence, Benedict. But I got enough circumstantial stuff to make the case a hundred proof."

Bill turned to Ruth who had been listening intently to Potts. "Ruth—"

She looked up to him.

"Ruth, do you think I killed your brother?"

She lowered her eyes and fluttered her fingers nervously. "I . . . don't know," she faltered. "I don't know what to think."

Bill took her hand and pulled her up from the chair. "Do you think I *could* kill him?" he demanded sternly.

She turned wildly from his eyes. "I don't know! I don't know! Maybe! Anything's possible!"

Potts crossed over to Bill. "It's a nice act you're putting on but I don't believe it."

"Potts, you dumb bastard. Finley and Laney have made a monkey out of you. Finley hired Laney to stink-bomb the opening of *Hour's End*. How do I know? Nick told me and so did Laney. Who's lying? Wait and see. Number one. Laney offered to name the murderer for five grand."

Nick Finley jumped to his feet and yelled, "Laney said that?"

"Sure." Bill smiled. "Laney said he'd turn you in, Nick, for a lousy five grand."

Nick glared at Bill and then wheeled swiftly on Laney. "You double-crossing sonuvabitch!" The squat Irishman tried to grab Laney but Potts and Nelson stopped him in time.

"You were blackmailing me," Nick yelled, "and dickering with Benedict at the same time!"

"What about it?" Laney muttered.

"I'll tell you what about it," Bill said to Laney. "When you read about Murray's death you saw your chance to blackmail Finley. You threatened him with telling the cops that he hired you to break up Leo's show. You figured that was good for at least a grand. But you discovered that Finley thought you knew more than you did. You jacked your price up to ten grand. He fell for it. From that time on, Laney, you were guessing. You guessed that if Nick Finley was willing to pay ten grand to hide a little thing like a stink-bomb, he must be afraid of something bigger. So you tried to get an extra five grand out of me by telling me that Finley murdered Murray." Bill walked over to where Nick was sitting, trembling and pale. "Nick, what did you do that you thought was worth ten grand to hide?"

Nick was silent. He kept playing with his tie and looking around the room as if it were a cage hemming him in.

"What about it, Finley?" Potts' voice boomed across.

Nick finally spoke. "I was to the Chicopee twice the night Leo was murdered. Once at eleven o'clock. Bill knew that. But he didn't know that I was there at eight, too. I was going to talk to Leo. Instead I saw Charlie Beach. I changed my mind and went away without seeing Leo. I swear to God! So help me!"

"That fits in nicely, Nick," Bill said. "You were afraid that maybe Laney followed you from Central Park and saw you enter the Chicopee at eight. Then you were scared that maybe Charlie Beach before he was killed told me he saw you, so you wanted to get rid of me. Two birds with one stone. Me and Laney. Laney kills me and then ducks out of sight to beat the murder rap. And for that you were paying me three hundred a week."

Potts cleared his throat. He flushed and chewed his gum savagely. "Bill . . ."

Bill grinned and turned to the detective. "No apologies."

"I'm sorry, Bill."

"That's all right, Potts. When you picked up Nick and Laney they had to combine against me in a modest little frame-up. It was their only way out."

Potts moved closer to Bill and addressed him as one professional to another. "Do you figure that Finley killed Murray, and Laney killed Charlie Beach?"

"No."

"No?" Potts leaned against a chair for support.

"No," said Bill again. "Someone else saw Charlie Beach that night and was frightened."

There was a tight silence in the room. Bill looked around the room. Laney and Finley were watching him darkly. Ruth sat at the edge of her chair, her fingers rolling a handkerchief ceaselessly.

"Who?" Potts' voice came harshly.

"Leo Murray's murderer."

Nelson, the little man, suddenly scratched a match across his thumbnail. The sound seemed explosive.

"Leo was murdered," Bill said, "by his wife." There was a tense silence. Potts started to say something but Bill interrupted. "A woman who passed off for years as his sister."

"You're crazy!" Ruth had risen from her chair and moved a step toward Bill. "Is this the best you can do? Finley gets you into hot water, and you're using me to pull out." She turned swiftly to Potts, her eyes lit with indignation. "You said you had enough on him. Why don't you take him away and stop this merry-go-round?"

"The kid you sent out of the room ten minutes ago, Ruth, wasn't your nephew. He's your son." Bill walked to the window and looked out. "You can find him at the reservoir, Potts," he said quietly. "Only you got to handle this thing right, Lieutenant, or I'll shut my trap right now."

"I'll handle it right," Potts said huskily. "Give." He nodded to Nelson. The little man took out a notebook.

Ruth bit her lips to keep them from trembling.

"Ruth, for ten years, you were married to Leo Murray. You were married secretly in Union City. You had a child."

Ruth clenched her fingers until her fists shone white. "He's lying," she cried out in a low voice.

Bill walked over to the bookcase and took out Lawson's book on playwriting. Behind it were the pamphlets. He showed them to Potts. "On child-training put out by the New York State Department of Health. I wired to Albany asking them if they had a record of sending such pamphlets to a Mrs. Leo Murray. They said yes and gave me the address. I hope you don't mind, Potts, but I signed the wire, William Benedict, Deputy Sheriff."

Potts kept a stony face. Ruth stared at the pamphlets.

"The address," Bill continued, "was in Manhattan. But no Mrs. Leo Murray lived there. I tried the local post office station. They had a forwarding address. To Jersey City. I went over. No one was home. I took the law, so to speak, in my own hands and broke into the house. I found this." Bill took a small bottle out of his pocket and put it on the table. "Exhibit A, Mr. Potts." He glanced at Ruth. She was looking at the bottle with fascination.

"This bottle contains a relatively common poison, aconite. Tasteless, colorless, slow-acting. How did you get hold of it, Ruth?"

"I never saw it before."

"You put enough in a glass of Scotch to kill me," Bill said relentlessly. "But, at the last minute, Sue came in and you got soft and changed your mind, so accidentally on purpose you spilled the Scotch before I had a chance to drink it. I wiped it up with this handkerchief." Bill took an envelope out of his pocket and tossed it to Potts. "You'll find the remains of the handkerchief and a chemist's report."

Ruth walked up to Potts boldly. "Let me see it!"

Potts showed it to her. She turned back to Bill. "It's your word against mine," she said passionately. "I don't know what you've got against me, but you're trying to frame me."

"Knowing Leo Murray, my hunch is that he refused to acknowledge you as his wife. For years this has been going on; then he decides to ditch Broadway and go to London to live. You're fed up with the deception. You want him to come out and tell the world who you are. He refuses. You go to my room and get into an argument with him. He threatens to throw you out. You lose your head and stab him. When commonplace people become murderers, they change, for the moment, into shrewd, clear, calculating animals. You wipe your fingerprints off my knife. You go downstairs and out of the hotel without being seen except by one poor wretch—Charlie Beach. For a couple days, Charlie, in his half-demented way, is loyal to you. He's read about Leo's death. He saw you in the vicinity at the time. He knows he'll be questioned—so he keeps away from the cops. But he gets worried. The cops are after him. He writes me a note telling me to meet him. You hear me say that on the phone to Potts. Charlie has to be gotten rid of before he tips me off about you. And this is where Frank Boley comes in. He found Charlie. How? I don't know. But Frank knew everything there was to know about the whole business. About you and Leo and the kid and the stabbing. Charlie is, therefore, killed. You sent yourself the John Wilkes Booth telegram hoping to hang suspicion on Nick Finley. You sent me the warning message. That was really foolish, Ruth. Only a woman would have said, '*Please do not try to find me.*' And the last bit of dope I needed came when Sue accidentally jabbed me with a swizzle stick. I was hit just about where Leo was. I'm his height, and I was bending. You stabbed Leo when he was bending. Didn't you, Ruth?"

She moved slowly to the couch and sat down wearily. When she spoke, they could hardly hear her. She said: "All guesses. Nothing . . . nothing else." She tried to smile.

"Thanks for the flattery, Ruth, but Frank Boley knew everything, and before he died he confessed."

A loud, shrill, unnatural scream came from Ruth. She jumped from the couch, ran to Bill and slapped his face over and over. "I don't care! I don't care!" Bill held her hands and pushed her back onto the couch. Hysterically, the words slipped through her lips. "He had money for everyone but his wife and son. His business manager had to embezzle money from him to support us."

"The Lionel Company . . ."

"Yes! And others! Every cent of the money Frank stole was our money. It went for the boy's education, for his clothes. Leo deserved to die!"

Ruth sat trembling like an old woman fighting to keep herself alive. "Leo wouldn't say I was his wife. He wanted someone who was brilliant and beautiful. I wouldn't give him a divorce. I was willing to live the way we'd been living until he said he was going to London. He called me at the office and told me he was at the Chicopee. He told me to come over."

"How'd ya get outta the office without Angus, the elevator man, knowing?" Potts asked.

"I walked downstairs. I used to do that often."

"And how'd'ya get up to Benedict's room and down again without being seen?"

"I don't know. I didn't call up from the desk. Leo told me the number of the room." Potts grunted. Ruth grabbed his arm fearfully. "No! Please! It wasn't premeditated. I didn't plan it. I was just going up to talk. And then he told me about London. And he was through with me. He wanted to take the boy with him. I pleaded with him. He wouldn't listen. . . ." She tightened her lips to control herself. The hysteria in her voice died away. She continued dully. "What Bill told you—about the rest—is all true. Only—I didn't want Frank to kill Charlie. I wanted to go to the police and tell them, but Frank said no. I shouldn't've listened to him." She became bitter. "If it wasn't for Frank, Charlie Beach'd be living today. And I wouldn't be sitting here. . . ." Her voice trailed away listlessly.

"It's too bad you didn't have more faith in Frank," Bill said after a while.

Ruth looked up at him sharply. "What do you mean?"

"If you had more faith, you'd've kept insisting that all I had was guesses."

"Bill!" Ruth was on her feet. "Frank confessed before he died!"

"Yeah . . . that *he* killed Leo."

Ruth started toward Bill again and fell to the floor, unconscious.

Potts had to wait for a matron to come up with an ambulance to take Ruth away. She was on a bed in another room, Nelson guarding. Laney and Finley were still there, looking impatient to get away.

"Well, Bill," Potts said expansively. "It's a nice job you done. She'll probably plead some unwritten law and with a good lawyer ought to be taking care of the kid in no time. As for you, if you want your agency back, I'll okay the application."

Bill grinned. "I got one more favor to ask you."

"Sure. What is it?"

Bill crossed the room to where Laney was lounging against a bookcase. "Make out you don't see the following bit of mayhem." Bill drew back quickly and slammed a right into Laney's jaw. He caught the gangster before he had a chance to fall and hooked another fist on his unpretty nose. Laney slid to the floor.

Potts scratched a package of gum. "Did you say something about a favor, Bill?"

By this time Bill was standing in front of Finley. "Now, Bill, don't be a mean guy," the producer was saying tearfully.

Bill contemplated Finley's soft face. "Come to think about it, Nick," Bill drawled. "I owe you five grand."

"Oh no, Bill! You don't owe me nothin'."

"Shall we say it's my fee for a little extra-curricular work?"

Nick smiled. "It ain't half enough, Bill."

"Don't red-apple me, Nick," Bill said curtly. "I'll keep the five because I deserve it. Suppose you take the other five that you might've given to Laney and see that Ruth Murray gets a good lawyer."

The phone rang. Potts answered. He turned to Bill. "It's for you."

"Hello . . ."

"Bill! Bill, darling. I've just found out. Potts forced the D.A.'s office to give him a warrant for your arrest. Get out of town, quick!"

Bill laughed.

"Don't laugh, Bill!"

"You can tell that dumb drugstore detective, Mister Potts, that Ruth Murray has confessed."

Bill glanced at Potts. The detective was chewing unhappily at the window making believe he didn't hear.

Bill let out a sudden yell. "What! No! Sue, for God's sakes! D'ya have to? That's not fair. But we were going to get married. You'll send me a fifty word night-letter explaining everything? Wait a minute! Sue!!!"

Bill hung up slowly. Potts turned, smiling hopefully. "What's a matter, Bill? She jilt ya?"

Bill sighed wearily. "If you want me you can reach me at my hotel."

"What's a matter, Bill? An illusion shattered?"

Bill looked at Potts as a bio-chemist might look at a dividing amoeba—with distance and objectivity.

"Potts," he said finally, "I've always been puzzled about you. How is it that sometimes you talk like a playwright, and sometimes like just an ordinary illiterate?"

The detective grinned and waved his chunky hand as airily as he could, "My friend," he said, "it's a trick of the trade. Like an actor puts on make-up, like a dame puts on the dog, like Grover Whalen wears a flower, so I—"

"So you, eh? And I figured you as a guy who thought a double-negative was something you put in a camera."

Bill left quickly.

The night-letter woke Bill at six the next morning.

BILL BENEDICT   NEWARK 540P 604P NL
HOTEL CHICOPEE
NEW YORK
MICHAEL WHYTE LATEST HOLLYWOOD PRO-
FILE DISAPPEARED FROM ROYALTY PICTURE
LOCATION IN THE HIGH SIERRAS THIS MORN-
ING STOP EXAMINER THINKS IT WOULD BE
GOOD NEWS SLANT IF DRAMA REPORTER

COVERED STORY STOP WHEN YOU RECEIVE
THIS I WILL BE SOMEWHERE BETWEEN THE
ADIRONDACKS AND THE ROCKIES STOP AM
NOT SURE MARRIAGE BEST THING ESPECIALLY
AS I HOPE TO MEET CHARLES BOYER ON COAST
STOP AS FAR AS I AM CONCERNED YOU ARE
STILL ELIGIBLE BACHELOR STOP CONGRATU-
LATIONS ON MURRAY CASE STOP CAN'T WE BE
FRIENDS? IF NOT WIRE COLLECT STOP LOVE
                              SUE HUXLEY

Bill looked sorrowfully at the virgin pillow next to his, sighed, turned out the light and returned to bed.

Murder in a Walled Town
Katherine Woods

Murder in Texas
Ada E. Lingo

The Strawstack Murder Case
Kirke Mechem

www.ingramcontent.com/pod-product-compliance
Lightning Source LLC
Chambersburg PA
CBHW020639250626
47154CB00008B/2745